DO ME A FAVOUR:

A Sweet Romance Novel

By

Rose Milburn

Cover designed by GetCovers

© All rights reserved

CHAPTER ONE

A Lunchtime Encounter

"Do me a favour," the face that suddenly appeared in front of Hazel begged her. "Please just keep looking directly at me and keep talking to me."

Hazel looked up from the plate on the table in front of her and found herself gazing directly into a pair of warm brown eyes just a few inches from her own.

"What the heck?" she exclaimed, leaning back a little as she realised that a smartly-dressed man, who she didn't know, had taken a seat in the chair opposite her and was just a little too close for comfort for someone she'd never seen before in her life.

"I'm sorry about this," the face with the friendly brown eyes apologised to her. "I'm just trying to keep out of the boss's way for a little while. He's been asking far too many questions about my private life and whether I'm already in a relationship with someone."

"Oh, really?" frowned Hazel, feeling somewhat confused.

"Yes," stated Mr Friendly Brown Eyes seriously. He had his elbow on the table and was propping his chin up on his hand, revealing a rather fancy chunky gold wristwatch, as he looked across at her. "You see, he's been trying to match me up with his only daughter, the 'lovely' Rebecca, and I'm definitely not interested in her. So, I told him I had a girlfriend and I was meeting her for lunch today."

While Mr Brown Eyes was speaking to her, Hazel could hear

the sound of some people making their way along the corridor outside the staff dining room. She estimated there must be about half a dozen of them; she could hear their muffled footsteps and their voices chattering, growing louder as they came near the wide-open door, then gradually fading away again as they moved further past.

After a few moments, the noise of the voices and footsteps died down completely, suggesting the group had moved along the corridor and round the corner to go somewhere else. Hazel watched as Mr Brown Eyes swivelled his head around to check behind him, left and right, that the coast was definitely clear, giving her a close-up view of his dark brown curly hair with golden highlights which just touched the collar of his crisp white shirt.

"Oh, it's okay, it looks as if he's gone," Mr Brown Eyes said as he turned his head back around to face Hazel, smiled at her and breathed out a big sigh of relief.

"What are you talking about?" Hazel asked him, still a bit bewildered as to what was happening. "Who's gone?"

"Oh, it was just the boss, the one who's been trying to play matchmaker between me and his daughter, but it's okay, he's gone away now. Sorry, I've got to go, maybe catch you later. See you around, Red," Mr Brown Eyes said as he began to stand up.

As she watched him slide sideways out of the chair and straighten all the way up until he reached his full height, Hazel realised that this Mr Brown Eyes person was quite tall, a good 6 feet, and slim, although he looked as if he worked out in a gym somewhere - probably a very expensive one – because she could tell he had a decent amount of muscle beneath the sharp three-piece suit, white shirt and red tie. She glanced down at his feet and saw that he was wearing sensible black socks and shiny, black slip-on shoes – she just knew he would be wearing shiny shoes. Men like him always did.

Hazel looked away from the expensive shiny shoes and back up at his face. Then, with a nonchalant wave of his hand and a smile that made his eyes crinkle a little at the sides and her frozen heart possibly defrost just a teeny bit, Mr Brown Eyes disappeared out of the staff dining room door.

With a quick glance to the left where the group of people he was trying to avoid were last headed, he made his escape rapidly in the opposite direction and she heard the tap-tap-tap of his expensive black leather shoes as he ran up the stairs to the next floor.

Hazel shook her head, still a little bemused at this performance and not entirely sure of what she'd just been unwittingly involved in.

Then she shrugged and carried on eating her lunch, such as it was.

A couple of ham sandwiches and a random, just about edible, tomato that she'd found in the back of the salad drawer of the fridge, weren't exactly the most exciting things she'd ever had for lunch but they were all she could find that morning. And she couldn't afford to go out to buy something from one of the local sandwich shops all the time, well hardly at all in truth, so she just had to make do as best she could, for the time being at least.

She'd decided on impulse that day to take fifteen minutes away from her office desk for once, so tired of trying to eat her lunch whilst still being tempted to glance at emails and pick up the phone when someone called her.

Hazel was sitting by herself in the staff dining room with its shiny red Formica tables and hard grey plastic chairs. Several other people were also in the room, in small groups of between two and maybe up to four or five, but no one was seated within a table or two of her so it was nice and peaceful. Or at least it had been until Mr Brown Eyes interrupted her.

On the whole, eating lunch in the staff dining room was not much better, certainly not much more comfortable, than staying at her desk if she was honest with herself but she acknowledged that at least there was a bit more space and there were plenty of white framed windows letting in lots of natural light.

And, more importantly, she was away from the temptations of the ringing phone and the computer with its endless emails pinging up and demanding to be answered. So, overall, she decided it was a good idea to take some time for herself at lunch that day and she would definitely do so now and again in the future.

Hazel finished eating her sparse lunch whilst eavesdropping in some amusement on the various conversations going on around her.

One group of people were discussing last night's latest reality television programme and who they thought was the best singer and deserved to get through to the next round; some were speculating on the new clients the company was trying to attract, while another group in the corner were discussing the merits of Botox and whether the results were worth spending the money on.

Meanwhile, two girls across the way from her were deeply engrossed in a discussion about a juicy new novel they were reading. She made a mental note of the title to mention this to Alice, the Paralegal who shared her office. She knew Alice was rather fond of a juicy new novel, though Hazel was definitely, absolutely, without any doubt, 100% not in the mood for romance in any way, shape or form these days. She'd had more than enough of all of that thanks to her former boyfriend, Adam.

CHAPTER TWO

Mr Brown Eyes

Ten minutes later, Hazel was back at her desk, carrying on with her work, typing out letters and completing lengthy conveyance forms, chock full of legalese, that she was pretty well certain no one really understood nowadays.

She had almost forgotten about the 'Mr Brown Eyes', who'd joined her uninvited at lunch, until she spotted him through the window, walking along the corridor outside her office. He was accompanied by an older, slightly portly, grey-haired, bespectacled gentleman of average height and a couple of others who were clearly hanging onto the grey-haired man's every important pronouncement.

This grey-haired man, presumably the boss he had mentioned earlier, said a few words to Mr Brown Eyes, who looked across at Hazel and clearly recognised her from the dining room earlier. He waved and grinned at her, showing the obligatory perfect pearly white teeth that she knew someone like him would always have, even if she suspected that they would owe more to high quality orthodontic work than good genetics. Being a polite sort of girl, Hazel obligingly waved back and smiled at Mr Brown Eyes.

The group moved further on but Alice, whose desk was right next to the corridor where that Mr Brown Eyes man had been standing, had noticed the interaction between the two of them and said, nodding her head in the direction that Mr Brown Eyes and the others had gone, "Ooh, look at you. Do you know that guy then?"

"I met him at lunch today," Hazel explained.

"Oh, really?" queried Alice, leaning forward, full of wide-eyed interest to learn more.

"Well, when I say I met him today," Hazel told her, surprised at Alice paying so much attention to what she was saying about this unexpected casual encounter, "I mean, to be precise, he appeared in front of me at lunch today in the staff dining room. He sat in the chair opposite me and asked me to keep looking at him and talking to him. Then he left when someone in the corridor had gone past. I couldn't see who it was because his head was in the way but I'm guessing it might have been that grey-haired man because he mentioned something about trying to avoid his boss."

"Oh, well!" exclaimed Alice, "I can tell you that the man, who you met at lunch, is the mysterious Mr James and the grey-haired man, the one who was with him in the corridor, is the Senior Partner, Mr Stevens.'

"All the single girls upstairs – and some of them who aren't even single - have had their eye on that Mr James since he started to work here a couple of months ago," Alice informed Hazel. "Rumour has it that Mr Stevens, the Senior Partner, whose office is on the top floor, has him in mind for his precious daughter, Rebecca, but the mysterious Mr James is giving absolutely nothing away. He claims he has a girlfriend but no one in the company has ever seen or heard any sign of her at all."

"Oh, tell me more?" Hazel enquired, really intrigued by all of this office gossip she had no idea was being discussed until Alice began telling her all about it. "How do they know there's no sign of a real girlfriend for this Mr James? How would they even *know* if he had a girlfriend?"

"Well," confided Alice. "They say he always seems to be available for work, whether it's very early in the morning, late on an evening, or even at weekends. If there's a tricky case on the go, he's *always* available. Vanessa even picked him up at home one day when he was waiting for his new car to be delivered from the dealers. She somehow managed to wangle her way into his apartment - using her womanly charms or something along those lines - and she said his place looks like a bachelor pad to her. And Vanessa should know, she's dated plenty of them."

Hazel breathed in a little, "Ooh, that's maybe a bit unkind."

"I'm not being bitchy," Alice defended herself, "It's a fact. We all know that. There aren't many single men in this building that Vanessa hasn't dated. But it seems the mysterious Mr James is immune to all of her charms. But perhaps not to yours? Go on then, tell me everything that happened during this lunchtime encounter with the mysterious Mr James from the top floor. I want all the juicy details!"

Hazel laughed. "Yes, well, I've pretty much already told you all about it," she answered. "He just appeared in front of me while I was eating my sandwiches in the staff dining room. He asked me to keep talking to him and said something about his boss wanting to match him up with his daughter, but he wasn't interested. Then he slipped away after a few minutes when the group of people he was trying to avoid had gone past, a group which I'm guessing probably included this Mr Stevens. That would make sense with what you said about Mr Stevens having Mr James in mind for his daughter, wouldn't it?"

Alice nodded.

"And, as you well know," Hazel said, "I'm not interested in that Mr James or anyone else for that matter, however handsome they may be. I'm off men for good, especially good-looking ones. I've had enough after the last one. I'm sticking to just doing my job and not socialising, particularly with attractive men. It's much, much safer that way."

Hazel had started her new job with their firm of solicitors about a year ago. She'd previously explained to Alice that she'd moved to the city, about 30 miles away from her family home, so she could put plenty of distance between herself and her last boyfriend, Adam, when their relationship broke up. Alice knew that this role also, of course, had a higher salary than the previous one she'd been doing near home and, therefore, helped her to pay off all the debt her former boyfriend had left her in.

"And how is Adam these days?" Alice's voice interrupted Hazel's thoughts about her home, her family and how badly Adam had treated her.

"Well, I hear that him and Jo are doing fine," replied Hazel, acidly. "They're expecting their second child already, apparently."

"From what you've told me about him, you're much better off out of it, Hazel," Alice reassured her.

"Yes, I know that but it still hurts when I think about it and, I swear, he's put me off men for life," she asserted.

On seeing Alice's disbelieving expression, Hazel added, "Okay, perhaps not for life but definitely for the foreseeable future. And there's one thing I do know, I will not be falling for just a pretty face again. They're the most dangerous ones of all."

"Okay, if you say so," agreed Alice, even though Hazel knew she was still secretly scouring through her list of friends and acquaintances for any eligible single men who might be suitable for her.

For some reason she couldn't understand even then, a full year later, Hazel had confided all her troubles to Alice, within just a few days of beginning work at the company.

She'd taken a liking to Alice from the very first time she'd set eyes on her after being directed to her desk in Alice's office on her first day at her new job.

Alice, a woman about ten years older than Hazel, so in her early thirties, had straight honey brown shoulder length hair, freckles and greeny-brown eyes a few shades lighter than Hazel's. Alice had greeted her warmly from the beginning, showing her where all the facilities, such as the coffee machine and staff toilets, were and letting her know that the girl she was replacing had been promoted and moved upstairs in the building, thereby putting Hazel's mind at rest about what might have happened to the previous occupant of the post she'd just commenced.

Alice had also explained all about company protocols such as when to take her breaks, what format to use for emails, the fonts they used for documents and all those important details that are often not explained to new starters until they make a mistake. And she answered any questions Hazel had, fully and patiently each time, making fitting into her new role so much easier than it would have been without that help.

After a couple of days, when Alice was telling her how she lived in a small, terraced house in the city with her husband and two children, she'd asked Hazel where she was staying. She ended up telling Alice not just where the block of flats was, at the far end of the high street, but also in floods of tears, the truth came tumbling out about the debt Adam had left her in and how devastated she really felt about having to move away from her family.

Alice took the time to listen carefully and ask all the right questions. She quickly grasped the situation Hazel was in, understood why she didn't want to tell her Mum and Dad and respected that decision.

From then on, Alice did everything she could to make things as easy as possible for Hazel. She would pay for coffees from the vending machine and occasionally buy their lunch or bring in lunch for them both, when she had leftovers from cooking for her family or items in the fridge that needed using up, and thereby releasing as much of the financial pressure on Hazel as she could.

Pretty much since then too, Alice had been on a constant quest to find an eligible bachelor for Hazel but, so far, her search had been unsuccessful. Though that didn't stop her from trying and neither did the fact that Hazel kept insisting she was staying away from men for good, or at least for the foreseeable future.

Hazel was not really much of a one for idle chitchat but then neither was Alice (unless it involved the goings-on upstairs on the top floor) which was perhaps why they got along together so well. Therefore, once the discussion about Mr James and how all the single girls upstairs were trying to attract his attention was over, they passed the afternoon in companionable silence deeply engrossed in their work, both downing tools at precisely ten minutes to five to pack up and go home.

After leaving their place of work, Alice returned to her little terraced house, husband and two young children while Hazel went back to her flat and, feeling a little sorry for herself after being reminded of Adam and what he had done to her, she treated herself to a Chinese takeaway at about 8 o'clock that evening.

While she was collecting her order, she made a mental note to add a ready meal for Saturday night to her shopping list so she wouldn't be tempted to splash out on her usual Saturday takeaway treat. She really couldn't afford to be throwing her cash around on takeaways, not if she wanted to pay off the debt Adam had lumbered her with in as short a time as possible.

CHAPTER THREE

Mr Brown Eyes Asks a Favour

A few days after their unexpected encounter in the staff dining room, Hazel was surprised to see Mr Brown Eyes suddenly appear in the doorway of her office at about 10 o'clock in the morning.

"Good morning, Red. And how are you this fine morning?" he asked cheerily, peering round the door frame and giving her one of his best toothy smiles. Hazel noticed the smile still made his eyes crinkle in that annoyingly attractive way.

She looked away from him. "I'm okay, thank you, hard at work as always. Is there something I can do for you?" she asked, realising she sounded a little harsher than she had intended, probably because he was an attractive man who was stirring up the very emotions that she had sworn she'd never let herself feel again, after Adam made such a fool of her.

Mr Brown Eyes smiled apologetically. "I need to ask you a favour. Will you come out to dinner with me?" he begged her.

As Hazel glanced back up at him in surprise at this unexpected development, he quickly explained, "We need to discuss a potential contract with a couple of clients and we're meeting them for dinner in the Cygnets Restaurant at the Swan Hotel. They're staying in the Swan, at the company's expense, while we discuss some further details of the agreement and I need someone to come along with me. You see, the clients are bringing their wives, Mr Stevens has invited his precious daughter, Rebecca, and I've told them I'll take my girlfriend along too. It seemed like such a good idea at the time. But there's just one slight problem: now I need to find a girlfriend."

"You'll be fine. You don't need me. I'm sure you must be able to find someone else to go there with you," Hazel insisted.

"No, that's the problem, Red," he answered. "I really won't be fine. That Rebecca person utterly terrifies me. Just imagine what she would be like if I upset her. Just imagine what her Daddy could do to me if I upset her. You wouldn't want bad things to happen to me," he gulped theatrically, "Would you?"

"It makes no difference to me," Hazel exclaimed.

"Oh, I would never have put you down as the heartless kind of girl who wasn't concerned one bit about her fellow man in his hour of need," Mr Brown Eyes pronounced solemnly, with a bit of a twinkle in his eye.

"I'm not heartless," she couldn't resist protesting but, knowing she was falling into the trap he'd set for her, Hazel added, "But that still doesn't mean I'm prepared to go out to dinner to impress these clients for you."

"Oh, please at least think about it. You see, Red," he explained sorrowfully, "I'm in a bit of a pickle. In a moment of madness, to stop him from talking about what a lovely couple myself and his daughter would make, I'd already told Mr Stevens I was dating a girl who works in the offices downstairs.'

"Then I picked you out the other day when I was trying to avoid him talking about her again at lunch. You were the only girl sitting by herself in the staff dining room, so I sat with you," he explained.

"Well, maybe you shouldn't have," Hazel told him firmly.

"I realise that now but, unfortunately, I did. Although I must say meeting you was a truly delightful experience and it really brightened up my day. However, you see, it turns out that Mr Stevens knows who you are. You're the only girl in the whole building who has long, red hair so he recognised you. It turns out his mother had red hair, or something along those lines, so he remembered who you are and which floor you work on. He pointed you out that afternoon, remember, when I waved at you?"

"Oh, yes, I remember," Hazel confirmed, recalling that Mr Stevens had indeed said something to this Mr Brown Eyes, prompting him to wave and smile at her.

"But now he thinks you're my girlfriend and he would like us to go out to dinner with the clients. He says having a pretty girl like you and his, as he describes her, 'charming' daughter with us at dinner will win the clients over and he has more chance of getting a good deal with them. Personally, I don't find Rebecca at all charming; black cats, broomsticks and whiskers on chins really aren't my thing, but each to his own I guess."

"It's still not my problem," Hazel responded sweetly, turning away from Mr Brown Eyes to face her computer and get on with her work.

"Think about it, please, Red," he pleaded. "Otherwise, I might lose my job. Upsetting Mr Stevens just isn't on. And upsetting Rebecca would be even worse for me. I'm under no illusions about that. I dread to think what her and her Daddy might do to me, under those circumstances, but I'm certain it wouldn't be pretty. And I'd hate for you to have that on your conscience, a lovely girl like you."

Hazel rolled her eyes at him but still had to try very hard to suppress a smile. She decided the word 'charming' might not suit that Rebecca girl but, against her better judgement, she had to admit that, beyond any doubt, it applied to this Mr Brown Eyes person.

He, meanwhile, pondered for a moment then added, "I know what I'll do. I'll come back at about 4 o'clock to ask you again after you've had time to think about it. Please think about it – and please say yes. The food will be delicious, the Cygnets Restaurant at the

Swan always is, I promise. And I really couldn't bear the thought of going to dinner with them and not bringing someone along to shield me from that awful Rebecca girl. I'm pretty sure she must spend every evening throwing eyes of frogs and toes of newts or whatever it is into her cauldron."

Hazel grinned, despite her best intentions, and, with a wink and a beaming smile at her, Mr James went on his way again, presumably up to the top floor where he worked as she could hear his footsteps as he ran back upstairs.

Once he'd gone, Alice came back into their office with two cups of coffee. She'd heard the end of the conversation and, after considering the issue for a few moments, she pointed out to Hazel, "Just think what you could get out of the mysterious Mr James if you agreed to go there for dinner tonight. You'll be treated to a lovely meal in a posh restaurant to begin with. The Swan Hotel is the swankiest in this city and I've heard the Cygnets Restaurant serves the most glorious food, though I could never even afford a bowl of their soup on my salary. And, now I come to think of it, perhaps you could even get Mr James to hand over some money for a new dress or something?"

"No, I really couldn't … could I?" The idea was truly starting to appeal to Hazel, as it was so long since she'd had sufficient spare cash to treat herself to a night out or a lovely new outfit. All she had been doing, for the past year, was barely making ends meet and gradually paying off the bills that Adam had left her with. The chance of a nice new dress and a delicious dinner in a really top-class restaurant was more than she had even dared to dream of for months.

"Of course, you could!" Alice responded eagerly, warming to the idea even more. "Who wouldn't like a nice new dress and the opportunity to go out for a lovely meal at the Swan? At the very least, it would be an experience to tell all of us other girls about and make us jealous. You'd be a total fool to turn it down, if you want my opinion."

"Hmmm, you may have a point," Hazel conceded, as she began to daydream about a tasty meal out and some nice new clothes to wear, neither of which she had been able to afford for far too long.

As the afternoon wore on, the idea of an enjoyable evening meal and the possibility of a nice new outfit began to sound more and more appealing to Hazel. As did the chance to have someone spend a bit of money on her for a change instead of her paying for everything, for both of them, the way she had all the way along the line with Adam.

She decided that, if Mr James did return, she might as well agree to go out with him.

CHAPTER FOUR

Dress for the Occasion

As he'd promised, mysterious Mr James did indeed come back at 4.00 pm to ask her again to come out for dinner with them.

"Please tell me you've thought about it and have agreed to go along to dinner with us tonight," he said solemnly, as he stood in the doorway of her office looking as totally dejected as his acting skills could manage. "I'll do anything you want. Just please say yes," he begged.

With a mischievous glint in her eye, Hazel pointed out that there could be a lot of things she would need for a night out in a posh restaurant like the Cygnets, particularly when she was expected to represent the company and impress both the boss and some wealthy potential clients. Not to mention to fit into the role of girlfriend for him, the upcoming lawyer, Mr James from the top floor of the building.

"Anything," he promised eagerly, then picking up on that glint in her eye, he added, "Well, within reason of course."

"And what would you consider to be reasonable?" she requested with an impish grin.

"Well, I'll pick you up and take you there," Mr James promised. "In my shiny, new Beamer."

"Taking me there is no big deal, I could easily get a taxi," she shrugged. "And what's a Beamer?"

"A BMW," he explained, clearly somewhat deflated. Hazel

guessed that people were usually delighted at being offered the opportunity for a ride in his brand spanking new car.

"Oh, right, I see, a BMW, that's some kind of expensive car, isn't it?" she asked, all wide-eyed innocence.

"Yes, it is an expensive car and a very nice car, if you're the sort of girl who's impressed by cars, which I guess you're not. So, erm, what else were you thinking that you might need me to provide you with so you will be able to go out for dinner with us tonight?" he asked.

Hazel made a show of deliberating for a moment (two can play at that acting game, she thought). "Oh, well, let me see, I might need some new clothes, for example," she suggested.

"But you must have something suitable to wear? It's smart casual dress code so a nice dress, perhaps a shawl or jacket and some court shoes or sandals would be fine. Maybe some gold or silver jewellery?" Mr James proposed. "Just some kind of smart, classy outfit. You look like the sort of girl who would have an extensive selection of smart and classy outfits."

"Hmm," she mused, "I really don't think I have a dress in my wardrobe, not here in the city anyway. I have clothes at home, at my Mum and Dad's, of course, but not in my flat. It's very small. There's no room for things that I won't wear very often. And, besides, I don't really get to go out anywhere, a takeaway now and then is about as exciting as my life gets, at the moment."

"Oh, that's a shame, I would have thought a nice, attractive girl like yourself would have loads of young men flocking around you eager to take you out for dinner on an evening," Mr James suggested.

"Well, I haven't," Hazel informed him adamantly and indeed it was true. There were no eager young men on the horizon, even if that was mainly because she had made it clear to them that she was not interested in going out on dates with them. She'd really had enough after Adam and was in no hurry to make the same mistake again.

"Oh, right, so you need some money to buy a dress? Well, that's no problem," he said, eagerly fishing in his brown leather wallet for cash. "And, as I'm paying for it, could I maybe recommend something green. In my opinion, green would go really well with your colouring, red hair and hazel eyes. You're a really pretty girl."

"Thanks, that's very kind of you and I'll think about your advice," Hazel replied, sounding as casual as she could, while enjoying the compliment and knowing perfectly well that green did indeed look good on her and was, in truth, her very favourite colour.

"And, of course, I'll need some sandals or smart shoes," she reminded him. "It's been pretty chilly most of the time since I came to work here in the city. It rained most of last summer, if you remember, and I don't really go out much on an evening anyway. I have had no need to bring summer sandals or court shoes with me until now, until you insisted on me going out for dinner tonight to impress the clients and do you a favour by pretending to be your girlfriend."

Mr James added another £30 to the pile of cash on the desk in front of her.

"And didn't you say something about needing to protect you from the unwanted advances of the boss's daughter?"

Another £20 note joined the money on the table.

"And I'd need a matching bag," she said, rather enjoying the opportunity to have someone spend money on her for a change, instead of having a boyfriend who was always finding ways to separate her from her cash. "Of course, I'll have to have a handbag to match the shoes, that is if you really want me to go out to dine at this very swish Cygnets Restaurant and impress these potential clients of yours?"

With a flourish, he added another £50 to the top of the pile. "Now that's got to be enough to convince you, surely?" he pleaded.

"Okay," she agreed, still sounding a little reluctant, "I guess I could go out for dinner with you."

"Oh, thank you, thank you, thank you," Mr James gushed and Hazel got the feeling that he really wasn't acting that time, he truly was extremely grateful, and mightily relieved, that he'd managed to talk her into going along and pretending to be his girlfriend. Maybe that Rebecca person really *was* a bit of a witch! It would be interesting to find out.

"It might be nice to go out somewhere for a change," she conceded, smiling at him.

"I promise I'll do my best to make certain you have a lovely time and I'll pick you up at 7 o'clock tonight. We'll need to be at the restaurant for 7.30," Mr James informed her.

Hazel smiled once more as she wrote down, on a yellow sticky note, the address of the block of flats where she lived. "I'll meet you in the lobby at 7 on the dot," she told him.

"Sure, of course, that's great. I'll meet you there at 7 in the lobby. And thank you again, Red," he said as he disappeared again, leaving nothing behind but a hint of musky aftershave and the memory of that impossibly white smile.

There followed an hour or so of earnest discussion between Alice and Hazel on the best place to go to look for a suitable dress and shoes at such short notice. They also had to decide what style of clothing might be appropriate for dinner with Mr James, Mr Stevens and the clients at the Cygnets Restaurant in the Swan Hotel. They finally agreed that a nice dress was a must but an internet search of local dress shops on Alice's phone showed they all closed at 5.00 pm or even earlier so that wasn't going to work, there just wasn't time even if Hazel slipped out early.

Eventually, Alice suggested that she try the nearby Outlet

shopping centre which Hazel agreed was an excellent idea. Alice recommended the names of a couple of shops to look out for and, as soon as she finished work, Hazel rushed to the Outlet before they closed at 6.00 pm, hoping against hope that she could manage to spend Mr James' money on some suitable attire.

CHAPTER FIVE

Hazel Goes Shopping

Keeping an eye on the time on her phone as the minutes ticked by, Hazel dashed from shop to shop in a fruitless search.

She decided she might have known that the clothes she liked wouldn't be in her size and, of those that were, she either wouldn't be very keen on them, or they wouldn't really be appropriate for an event such as the one she was due to attend. There was a green dress she found that just about fit her, but it was a bit frumpy and a little too short, and a lovely pair of jeans that Hazel would have been delighted with at any other time, but they were hardly suitable for the 'smart casual' dress code at the fancy Cygnets Restaurant.

Eventually, when she was getting really desperate, a green and blue patterned dress with a matching full-length coat caught Hazel's eye on a mannikin in the front window of a shop. She stopped and gazed at it, taking in every detail. It was truly beautiful – but she was certain it would be more than she could afford, even if it was the mysterious Mr James' money she was spending rather than her own.

Hazel went inside the shop and, trying not to draw the attention of the staff, she tiptoed over to look at the price tag hanging from the coat. It said £70. Checking all over the dress, she couldn't find another price ticket anywhere but then one of the impossibly glamorous shop assistants, obviously hoping for a sale, walked purposefully up to her and asked if she needed any help.

"It's beautiful, isn't it?" the Shop Assistant whispered softly to Hazel, when she saw her eyes still looking longingly at the outfit, "And it would look so good on you, madam. You'd really suit it."

"Thank you," she smiled, still unable to tear her eyes away from the outfit.

"It's a bargain, isn't it, for £70?" the Assistant prompted her.

"It is," Hazel agreed, finally managing to look away from the outfit and directly at the Sales Assistant, who she saw was wearing a name tag with 'Julie' on her lapel.

As 'Julie' was standing right there beside her and eager to help, Hazel thought she may as well ask her, "So how much is the dress that goes with it?" She was hoping against hope that it wouldn't be another £70 because, of course, she also needed a pair of shoes with a matching bag.

She didn't think the large black hold-all she usually carried about with her would go down too well in a flashy restaurant like the Cygnets, where Mr James and Mr Stevens were taking their clients to impress them.

"That's the price for the set," the Assistant, Julie, confirmed to her. "For both the dress and the coat."

"Oh, really?" breathed Hazel, hardly daring to believe her luck.

"Yes, they're a real bargain, aren't they? They're new in, part of a cancelled order, I believe. Now, let's see if we can find your dress size. It's only limited stock. Let me see, you must be a size 14, I would guess?"

"Yeah, about that," Hazel agreed.

The Shop Assistant looked carefully through the rail and picked out a size 14 in both the dress and the coat.

Hazel took the outfit from her and walked into the changing room, crossing her fingers tightly, hoping that the items would fit.

With a glance at the time on her phone, she hurriedly took off her sensible work clothes of long black skirt and grey shirt and tried the dress on, coming out into the aisle between the rows of changing rooms to get a look at herself in the full-length mirror. Like many girls, she wasn't terribly keen on viewing herself in the changing room mirror but knew she had to on this occasion, she couldn't take the chance of finding the dress didn't hang correctly on her when she got it home because she really had nothing else in her wardrobe that she could wear instead.

"Oh wow," said Julie, the Shop Assistant, peeking through the doors leading into the fitting rooms, "That looks so good on you, madam." Hazel did a twirl in front of the mirror as the Assistant brought over a long, hand-held mirror so she could see the back of the dress firstly and then, when she slipped the long-line matching coat over the top, see how it looked with that too.

"Are you happy with them?" Julie asked.

"Mmm, yes, I'm delighted," Hazel confirmed, still twirling about in front of the mirror. The skirt of the dress flared out beautifully as she moved about

"Is it for a special occasion?" Julie asked her.

"I'm going out for dinner at the Swan," Hazel informed her, looking at the back of the dress and coat in the mirror again. "For a work event."

"Oh my, that's a fancy place but you'll fit right in wearing that outfit," smiled the sales girl.

"Now, is there anything else you'll need, madam?" she asked.

"I could really do with a pair of shoes and a matching handbag," Hazel confessed.

"Yes, I see," said Julie, looking down at Hazel's sensible, chunky flat black boots and large black hold-all. "Can you wear heels, madam?"

"Yes, of course I can, these boots are just comfortable for work," Hazel explained.

The Shop Assistant smiled conspiratorially, "I have just the thing. What shoe size would you be?"

"A 5 or a 5 and a half, depending on the fit," she answered.

Julie walked into the storeroom to the rear of the shop and came out with a box containing a pair of size 5, grey snakeskin patterned, slingback shoes with two and a half inch heels. "These have just come in today," she informed Hazel, taking them out of the box. "We will be putting them out on display for tomorrow when the shop closes tonight but they'd be ideal for you and there's a matching handbag," she added triumphantly.

Hazel slipped the grey slingback shoes on and the Assistant helped her to tighten the strap one notch so they fit her like a glove. The handbag offered was a perfect match to the shoes – with a snakeskin patterned centre panel – and was just big enough to be useful but not so big that it would get in the way or overpower the outfit either.

"You look lovely, madam," Julie assured her and Hazel had to admit she did feel quite special, all dressed up in her finery.

Altogether, the cost of the outfit, shoes and bag was heading towards a week's salary to Hazel but she guessed Mr James could afford it as he was a well-paid up-and-coming young lawyer who worked on the top floor of the building.

Once she had paid for her purchases and they'd been carefully wrapped in tissue paper by the Assistant, Hazel rushed home, threw off her clothes in an untidy heap in the bathroom and jumped straight into a warm shower. She really was pushing it for time.

After rapidly towelling herself dry, she blow-dried her hair as best she could in the time available. With a natural wave to it, her hair always managed to look somewhat wayward at the best of times and, as it was still partly wet, Hazel knew that meant it would go its own merry way even more than usual as the evening progressed. But there was nothing she could do about that, she didn't have time to dry it any further. She slapped on some make-up, taking care mainly that she didn't overdo the eyeliner or blusher, sprayed herself with perfume at top speed and put on the outfit she'd just bought, grateful that she'd managed to find something that fit perfectly for once.

Then she put on the shoes and took the paper tissue stuffing from the bag, replacing it with her purse, some bits of make-up and the £50 left over from the cash Mr James had given her to purchase her outfit. Under the circumstances, she thought it was reasonable to expect him to pay for the clothes. Asking her to go out to dinner that same night was very short notice and she genuinely had nothing appropriate with her in the city, but it was only right to give him back the rest of the money. Her conscience would never allow her to even think of hanging onto it, no matter how tight her finances were. It just wouldn't be right.

Looking at herself in the mirror, Hazel thought how strange it is that you can spend ages looking for the right outfit, weeks or months in advance of a special event, without ever finding anything that is properly suitable and sometimes simply perfect clothes just come along when you have only a minute's notice, although she knew the Assistant had been a marvellous help.

Hazel realised she would never have managed to pull her outfit together in time without that wonderful Sales Assistant and she resolved to go back to the shop, as soon as she could manage, to say how grateful she was for the help the Assistant had given her.

CHAPTER SIX

Mr James Collects Hazel

All washed and brushed up, primped and preened (or as near as she could be in something less than an hour), Hazel pressed the button to summon the elevator, ready to meet the mysterious Mr James downstairs in the lobby at 7.00 pm prompt.

As she travelled down, she put her hand up to her neck, realising that she'd forgotten to wear a necklace, but she really didn't have time to go back and find one. She'd promised Mr James that she'd meet him at 7 in the lobby and didn't want to be late.

Never mind, she decided, the outfit looked good in its own right anyway, there was no real necessity to wear any jewellery with it.

To her surprise, when she reached the lobby and stepped out of the elevator five minutes early, she discovered Mr James was already there waiting for her, leaning casually against a pillar on the far side of the foyer and, she had to admit, looking even better than he had the first couple of times she'd met him. She was pretty much convinced that the suit was just a little bit sharper and the shoes a teeny bit shinier even than she'd seen them before.

He wasn't watching in her direction, as there were a number of elevators in the building and he wouldn't know which one she would be coming out of, so Hazel was able to sneak up behind him. As she got closer, she realised he was smelling of some gloriously expensive cologne with many different perfume notes. It wafted over to her even though she was still a few yards away from him. She just knew he would smell of ridiculously expensive cologne on an evening like this, men like him always did.

To her dismay, she felt the same fluttering in her stomach that she'd felt when she first met Adam. She carried on walking towards the mysterious Mr James and pushed the feeling away back down inside her. She wasn't going to fall for that old trick again. Work, she was focussed on work for the next two years, till she'd paid off the debt and built up her savings again, and even then she was going to be very careful who she got involved with and not be taken in by a handsome face ever, ever again.

Adam had totally cleaned out her savings with his 'let's go here and let's do this fun thing or that fun thing' attitude. Depending on his whims, the 'fun thing' could be going bowling or to the cinema, for a meal out, a day at a theme park or a week in Benidorm. It had happened over and over again in the three years Hazel had been with him, there was always something fun that Adam thought they should do.

And every time Hazel had had to pay for whatever fun activity it was that he'd decided they should do that day or that week.

Of course, Adam always had a plausible excuse: he'd left his wallet behind or he was a bit short of cash that particular month or he needed his money to buy his mum a birthday present. Thinking back over their time together, Hazel had worked out months ago that he must have used the excuse about his mum's birthday at least 4 or 5 times in the three years she'd known him, what an idiot she felt for not realising what he was like.

Of course, he always promised he would make it up to her but, one day, when she went to pay a bill with her debit card and was shocked to discover that she didn't have enough funds in her account to cover it, she suddenly realised what a twit she'd been and told Adam the relationship was over.

Now she was concentrating on work, trying to get her finances back on an even keel and doing her best to ensure she'd never be such a total idiot over any man – no matter how good looking he was – ever again.

Just three months after she parted company with Adam, while she was still discovering debt management letters and unpaid bills coming in the post with her name on them, she found out he had moved in with a girl called Jo and they were expecting their first child together.

It still hurt Hazel that he'd promised her for three years that they would set up home and start a family - when he was ready to settle down and they had managed to save up some money to pay for it, of course. But, within weeks of being with his new lady friend, he had moved in with her and she was expecting a baby.

Anyway, she told herself, she was well over Adam now and, as Alice had said, so much better off without him even though it was a hard lesson she'd had to learn. There was no way she was ever going to make the same mistake again.

When Hazel reached within a pace or two of Mr James, he must have heard her footsteps. He turned around and smiled – a bright smile that made his brown eyes twinkle in a very attractive way.

She had to admit he was a very good-looking man and, up close, she decided that perhaps she had been a bit unkind in judging him as having loads of orthodontic work. There was a barely noticeable crookedness to one of his front teeth that suggested maybe the dazzling smile really was down to good genetics instead of a top-class orthodontist.

Whatever the truth, something about him seemed to keep lighting up the flame of hope inside of her and that flame kept threatening, against her will, to defrost her frozen heart.

Hazel securely stamped down the glow of hope that seemed to grow inside her whenever she met the mysterious Mr James. She reminded herself that she was not going to make a fool of herself again over a man, any man, especially a good looking one with eyes that twinkled the way his did. They just weren't worth the heartbreak.

Mr James said, "Hello, Red. And may I say you look very lovely tonight," looking her up and down from head to toe and clearly admiring her new outfit.

He took hold of her hand, which seemed to send an electric spark along her arm and right down to the warm glow that kept flaring up inside her. And, judging by the way he breathed in deeply, the touch they shared had a similar effect on him. Hazel took a deep breath of her own and with a superhuman effort she wrestled that flame back down into its box again as Mr James led her outside into the street to introduce her to his BMW, a shiny green car, which he told her was a BMW 8 series Gran Coupe.

While nodding at him and trying not to look overly interested, Hazel finished off the details in her head, "And, by the looks of it, in Sanremo Green Metallic with black full merino leather interior. Goes from 0-62 in 3.9 seconds and reaches the heady heights of 26.2 miles per gallon."

Her younger brother, Tommy, had drummed into her head for the past few years all the details of the various ridiculously expensive cars he wanted to buy when he grew up and this was one of his favourites.

"Oh, it's a nice colour," she replied, sounding deliberately unimpressed.

"Sanremo Green," Mr James informed her.

Ah ha, so she'd been right, thank you, little brother. Hazel nodded, "Yeah, it's a nice colour."

"Thanks," he said, then added abruptly, "I've got something here that I think would be perfect for you to wear tonight."

He took a black velvet bag from the top pocket of his suit jacket and lifted from it a heavy golden pendant with a large green stone.

"It will look beautiful with that dress and jacket," he claimed.

"Oh yes, it matches the green in the dress really well. It's very pretty. Is it real?" she asked, trying in vain to get a proper look at it, as he placed it around her neck and fastened it at the back.

"18 carat gold and emerald surrounded by 12 brilliant cut diamonds," Mr James confirmed but shut down any attempts of hers to ask any further questions about it.

He opened the passenger side car door for her and closed it when she was safely seated inside, then drove them across town. He parked outside the Cygnets, which was clearly a *very* expensive restaurant. Hazel could see it was all shiny glass and carefully concealed lighting, with impeccably dressed staff waiting with bright white napkins folded over their arms, ready to attend to their guests' every single whim.

At that point, while they were still parked outside the restaurant, she remembered about the £50 remaining from the money Mr James gave her for her outfit. She took the unspent notes out of her new handbag and held them out to him, explaining what they were.

He looked a little surprised and protested that it was fine, that she should keep the change, but Hazel insisted on him taking it back, stating that he'd given her the cash to buy an outfit and she'd done that. She told him strongly that she would feel really bad if she kept the money she hadn't used, so he nodded an acknowledgement and said thanks.

Hazel sincerely hoped that Mr James or even Mr Stevens were claiming for her evening meal and drinks on their expenses and she wouldn't regret giving him back the cash. She really didn't want to spend the next six months doing the washing up for the restaurant after work, to settle up for her part of the meal, and she was totally convinced that, on her salary and with the debts she was paying off, there was no way she could afford to pay for a meal here outright. It looked a long, long way out of her price range, but then the local sandwich shop was way out of her price range most of the time these days.

CHAPTER SEVEN

Out for Dinner

As Hazel and Mr James entered the restaurant, the maître d' welcomed him by name, "Good evening, Mr James," and escorted them through to one of the smaller rooms. She discovered that Mr Stevens, a girl, presumably his daughter, Rebecca, as well as some people who she guessed were the clients and their wives, were already seated at a secluded table near the back wall.

Rebecca had quite a large pointy nose and steel rimmed spectacles, she was wearing a bright orange wrap-around dress with a lilac stole. The first client, a tall grey-haired man was dressed in what was clearly an expensive, if slightly ill-fitting, suit, while the second, a smaller gentleman, was wearing brown trousers with a grey checked jacket. One of their wives was a buxom lady while the other was much smaller in both height and build. They were both wearing designer labels and sensible shoes.

Mysterious Mr James asked Hazel what she would like to drink and, being determined to keep her wits about her, she opted for diet coca cola, which came served in a tall glass with lots of ice and slices of lemon and lime.

While they all perused the offered menus, Mr Stevens and the clients discussed the merits of the various options on offer. Mr James said he would have the melon sorbet for his starter and recommended it to the others. Hazel decided she would try the sorbet too and then she requested the lemon chicken for her main course.

Rebecca wanted snails in garlic butter (or escargots de bourgogne as they were labelled on the menu) and rare beef, which somehow didn't surprise Hazel one bit. Meanwhile the rest of those in attendance opted for more conventional options such as fruit juice, vegetable soup and roast beef or pork. Mr Stevens ordered the meals and two bottles of wine and Mr James asked for a jug of water for the table since he was driving.

They were sipping drinks and waiting for their starters to be brought across to the table when Rebecca Stevens, Mr Stevens' precious daughter, who Hazel could see had indeed taken something of a shine to Mr James, asked them coldly, "How did you two meet? I'm guessing it wasn't at work as the different floors don't usually mix."

She clearly thought Mr James was slumming it, hanging around with a lowly second floor girl like Hazel.

"We met in an aqua aerobics class," Hazel responded, smiling sweetly at Mr James as he snorted, in a quite ungentlemanly manner, into his drink.

"You were doing aqua aerobics?" Mr Stevens asked. His tone of voice did not exactly suggest approval at one of his finest young male lawyers indulging in aqua aerobics as a way of keeping fit.

Turning away from the view of Mr Stevens and his daughter, Mr James looked daggers at Hazel as she gazed innocently at him. However, he quickly regained his composure and responded, "Yes, erm, erm, it's important to keep fit, don't you think?"

"And aqua aerobics is one of the most fun ways of doing it, isn't it darling?" smiled Hazel, encouragingly.

Mr James muttered something unintelligible into his glass of mineral water but, as he looked at her over the rim of the glass, Hazel thought she could still detect a hint of amusement, and possibly even admiration, at her for not only having the absolute nerve to conjure up a response like that but then to actually say it out loud in front of those important people.

"Oh, I've just realised," said Rebecca, clearly suspecting that something wasn't right with their relationship, "You haven't formally introduced us to your lady friend, Mr James."

"Oh, of course, where are my manners?" Mr James replied, looking at Hazel and then round the table at the other guests. "This is Mr Stevens, our Senior Partner, you must know him already from work, this is his, erm, his lovely daughter, Rebecca, and these two gentlemen are our hopefully new clients, Mr George and Mr Burns with their respective spouses, Jane and Chris."

Mr George, the larger of the two gentlemen, introduced himself as Peter and smiled warmly at her. Mr Burns, the smaller gentleman, told her his name was Bobby and said how he was pleased to make her acquaintance, whilst their wives, Jane and Chris, murmured similar responses.

"And this lady is?" questioned Rebecca, looking pointedly at Hazel.

"Erm, as you said, my lady friend, erm, erm, Red, as I call her," Mr James replied.

Taking pity on him because Rebecca, clearly one of those people who had wanted for nothing in her life and thought she was automatically entitled to anything she did want, was making her teeth itch, Hazel jumped in. "I'm Hazel. Hazel Brookes. And yes, I know, before anyone else says it, my name sounds like a second-rate holiday resort. But he – Mr James – usually calls me Red."

"Mr James?" queried Rebecca, suspiciously, "Surely you are on first name terms with your boyfriend?"

"Benjamin," he cut in, "Of course, she knows my name is Benjamin."

"Of course, it is," Hazel responded quickly, "He's Benjamin." Then focussing a laser-like gaze on Rebecca, who was really beginning to grate on her very last nerve, she added firmly, "*My* Benjamin!"

In an attempt to soothe any ruffled feathers after that exchange, Mr Stevens turned the conversation to more mundane matters such as the weather.

Soon the waiting staff began serving the starters to their table and a couple of the others in the room who were ready to order at the same time.

One of the waitresses was carrying a basket of bread rolls, individual portions of butter and a pair of tongs. Suddenly, an elderly man at a nearby table pushed his chair back to stand up, not realising that the waitress was right behind him. He knocked everything out of the girl's hands. The basket went flying off to her left and the rest of the items shot in every other direction.

At that moment, Rebecca was returning from the ladies' restroom. She pushed haughtily past the waitress crouching down in her way, standing on a couple of the bread rolls and squashing them into the carpet.

The girl was hugely embarrassed and bright red in the face, trying to track down all the missing items and pick them up from where they'd rolled across the carpet. Hazel collected a couple of bread rolls and several packs of butter from near her seat. She put them back in the basket, with a sympathetic smile to the young waitress, while Mr James, Benjamin, located most of the other missing bits such as the tongs and the few remaining bread rolls and gave them back to the girl too.

As they both leaned across to drop the final couple of items into the basket so the waitress could take them away, Mr James smiled and winked an acknowledgement to Hazel for being prepared to help, whispering, "Thanks, Red. As my Mum always told us, it costs nothing to be kind."

After that excitement, the carpet was swiftly cleaned up by other restaurant staff, the bread rolls were replaced by another waitress and the meal passed without further incident.

They consumed their first courses, really enjoyed the main courses, admiring the skills of the chef and discussing other places, both good and bad, where they had dined out previously. Then the conversation turned to a discussion on the details of the contract they were negotiating while they ordered dessert before they finished the evening with excellent coffee, sugar and cream all round.

When Hazel popped to the bathroom as staff were serving the coffee, she looked at her outfit in the full-length mirror and thereby got her first proper view of the pendant that Mr James had placed around her neck.

It was truly gorgeous, a huge pear-shaped emerald, set in what she assumed to be – as he'd said - a diamond surround, hanging from a heavy, long gold chain. Mr James was absolutely correct, it did indeed match the emerald green swirls in her outfit beautifully. They could have been chosen to go together.

And, although she wasn't at all conceited, she was pleased that she had scrubbed up as well as she had in the short time available and, therefore, felt she could hold her own in the company of Mr Stevens' expensively clad, if rather ill-humoured daughter, Rebecca.

The very thought of Rebecca made her shudder. She could quite see why Mr James wanted someone to shield him from her advances and she decided to hurry back to continue with the role of protective girlfriend for Mr James, or Benjamin as she was having to remember to call him whenever she spoke to him.

She had to admit that the expression 'my Benjamin' had quite a nice ring to it.

Nope, she reminded herself, we are not, I repeat not, going down that route again, my girl.

She returned to her seat and, remembering the purpose of Mr James inviting her out to dinner, she smiled protectively at him to send a message to Rebecca as she sat back down.

To Hazel's relief, after the coffee and mints, Mr Stevens paid for the whole meal, along with a respectable tip for the staff, using his credit card.

They all said their goodbyes as Mr George and Mr Burns agreed to discuss matters between themselves and relay any questions to Mr Stevens, if they required further details of the deal he had promised, then come back to him with a final decision.

The clients and their wives retired to the Swan Hotel lounge for a few drinks and Mr Stevens shook Mr James' hand warmly to say thank you for his support and assistance during the evening, while Rebecca scowled at Hazel behind his back before they left in a taxi.

CHAPTER EIGHT

Returning Home

As he drove Hazel back across the city to her block of flats, Mr James, who of course she now knew was called Benjamin, said to her, "Thank you for bailing me out there with the lovely Rebecca, Red, erm I mean Hazel. I'm sorry for dropping you in it by not asking your name or telling you mine when I picked you up."

"It's okay," she laughed, "I think we handled it pretty well, on the whole. I enjoyed getting one over on Rebecca and I can quite see why you're trying to keep her at arm's length. People like her need to know they can't always have everything they want."

"They do," he agreed but added, "I still think it was a bit mean of you, though, telling them we met during an aqua aerobics class. I nearly choked on my mineral water and Mr Stevens and indeed his 'delightful' daughter, Rebecca, might never look at me in the same way again."

"That might not be such a bad thing in Rebecca's case," Hazel pointed out.

"Very true," grinned Mr James. "That's a really good point! Every cloud and all of that."

"And, anyway, it was pretty funny," chuckled Hazel. "Your face was a picture when I mentioned aqua aerobics, but I was only getting my own back because it was quite mean of you to drag me into your lies," she added. "Telling them I was your girlfriend then talking me into dining out with these people I had never even met to protect you from Rebecca."

"Yeah, I know, I'm sorry, Red. But I had to do something to keep her away from me. And I can see that you're a nice girl, you wouldn't want someone like Rebecca to get her long, sharp claws into me, would you? I'm a sensitive sort of chap. She gives me the heebie-jeebies," he said plaintively.

"Yes, she does have a bit of an air of being totally spoilt, expecting her own way all the time and probably turning nasty if she doesn't," agreed Hazel.

"Exactly, and can you imagine what Daddy would do to me if I turned down her advances? It's much better to let them both think that I already have a girlfriend. It makes it much easier to keep her at arm's length. Personally, I'd prefer a barge pole but I think her Daddy might notice," he laughed.

"Having met her, I can see why you feel the way you do," Hazel said solemnly, trying not to giggle at the image of a smart-suited Mr James attempting to keep Rebecca well away from him by means of a barge pole, which she guessed was some sort of long implement similar to the pole used during the pole vault. Although that was purely a guess, she had never actually encountered a real-life barge or indeed an actual barge pole in her life so far.

"Penny for your thoughts, Red," Mr James said, having glanced across at her a couple of times, as he was driving, and seen the various shades of amusement and deep consideration (as she thought about what a barge pole might look like) show in her expressions but she shook her head and didn't answer. She really didn't think he'd appreciate her letting him into the secret image inside her head of him holding a vicious, snapping, fire-breathing Rebecca at bay with a long pole, like some sort of smart-suited Saint George.

Mr James remained quiet after that and drove up to the front of her block of flats. He parked close to the kerb, got out of the car, walked around while she was fumbling in the footwell for her handbag and opened the passenger door for her.

"Will you be okay from here, Red?" he asked, as she climbed out of the car.

"Yes, thanks, I'll be fine," she assured him, walking across the pavement and up to the front entrance of the flats away from him.

She gave him a brief wave, at the top of the steps, and he acknowledged her with a wink and a grin then got back into his car.

CHAPTER NINE

The Pendant

Trying not to think about how mysterious Mr James made her feel when he was in close proximity to her, and she could smell that glorious aftershave and see the way his eyes crinkled when he smiled and hear his warm, baritone voice softly speaking to her, Hazel walked across the lobby.

She pressed the button to summon the elevator but, just as it arrived at the ground floor and she knew the doors were about to open, she heard heavy footsteps behind her and realised that Mr James, Benjamin, was running across the lobby towards her.

Thinking he was regretting leaving her and was about to ask her for another date or declare his undying love or something along those lines, as in all the best romantic films, she forgot her resolution not to get involved with a man for a good long time and turned towards him with a wide smile on her face.

When he caught up with her, for one moment, Mr James looked deep into her eyes as he reached up and softly brushed her cheek with the tips of his fingers.

In that moment, it felt as if the whole world was standing still for Hazel. Nothing existed in the entire universe, apart from those warm brown eyes gazing into hers, the alluring scent of his aftershave, his soft breath on her cheek and the loud beating of her own heart in her ears.

For an instant, she thought he was going to lean over and kiss her there on the spot, but the spell was broken when a young guy in a black and white tracksuit pushed past her to get into the lift and Mr James moved back.

At that time, she felt the small beacon of hope burning brighter inside her again but, before she could move to squash it back down herself, Mr James did it for her instead.

He seemed to remember the real reason he had returned to her and said curtly, "The necklace. I almost forgot about it. The necklace," and he reached up to take it from her neck. Seeing her shocked expression at the way he was behaving, he added a clarification of sorts, "It belonged to my mother."

Hazel put her hands up behind her neck, unfastened the clasp herself and handed the pendant over to him. He gently caressed it, indeed it seemed he couldn't tear his eyes away from it and, with his hand visibly shaking, he put the pendant back into its velvet bag then placed it in the top pocket of his suit jacket and stepped away from her.

Suddenly, obviously feeling as if he owed her some better kind of an explanation than he'd provided so far, Mr James stopped in his tracks, turned around again and looked back at her.

"It was my Mum's," he said apologetically. "The last thing I ever bought for her. She told me it was beautiful and I should give it to my special girl when I find her. I always carry it with me, it makes me feel that my Mum is still with me in some way.'

"The outfit you bought was such a glorious emerald green colour, I knew it would look fabulous with her pendant. And it did. You looked so lovely. It was a real pleasure to take you out to dinner tonight and thank you for that. You did so well to stand up to Rebecca the way you did and I really enjoyed the evening. All in all, you're quite a girl, Miss Hazel Brookes, and thank you again, thank you ever so much for a truly wonderful evening."

He bobbed his head, smiled his bright sparkly smile at her and turned to walk off yet again.

Hazel stood with her back to the wall, just beside the elevator doors, taking in several deep breaths and watching him as he made his way across the lobby before disappearing through the front doors and into the darkness yet again.

Once she was sure he'd definitely gone out of the building and into the cold night air outside and wasn't coming back this time, she turned and pressed the button for the elevator once more.

She rode up to the third floor, the elevator doors opened up and she walked along almost to the end of the corridor to reach her flat, punching the number to unlock the door into the keypad. Then she went inside and closed the door behind her, moving across and dropping her bag onto the tiny sofa that they'd managed to squeeze into the room.

Hazel could feel the heaviness of the meal still sitting in her stomach. She must do some extra exercise tomorrow to make up for it, she was turning into a right little porker as her Dad used to affectionately call her. At the time, in her early teens, it used to really annoy her, but now she understood that it was just gentle teasing from a Dad, who loved her very much, and he didn't mean it to be hurtful at all. She wished she could see her family every day the way she did before she moved to the city, and she wouldn't even complain one tiny bit about him saying she was turning into a little porker.

Anyway, right now she was just too tired to even so much as think about exercise and burning off those calories from the meal. The whole evening had really taken it out of her emotionally. That Rebecca person was horrid and really draining – and so, so demanding. No wonder Mr James – Benjamin – wanted someone to help him keep her at arms' length – or at barge pole's length, whatever one of them might be.

Hazel smiled to herself when she remembered the way Mr James had looked at her when they'd shared a joke over dinner. His eyes had done their crinkling at the sides in a very attractive way thing, she'd noticed again.

Then she realised what she was doing and no, no, no, no, no, she was *not* going to go down that route again. She'd had more than enough of all of that with Adam. She would not let it happen to her again.

She hurriedly slipped off the coat and dress then sat down on the sofa, admiring them laying by her side. She had to concede that those garments were beautiful, some kind of silky polyester material she guessed, blue and emerald-green swirls on a white and grey background. She took off the shoes, pale grey leather, with mid-height slim heels. They were both good purchases, she thought, as indeed was the matching bag.

With a smile, she admitted to herself she'd done well there. Thank you, mysterious Mr James.

With that thought, her mind wandered again to his strange behaviour downstairs in the foyer. Running after her to collect the pendant from her. She didn't blame him at all, it was clearly worth quite a lot of money – but there was obviously more to it than just its material worth. It must have a lot of sentimental value to him too.

Thinking back, she realised what he'd said about it being the last gift he'd ever bought for his mother and how she wanted the pendant to go to a special girl who would enjoy it.

Tears sprung to her eyes as she thought about Mr James losing his mother and she swallowed hard at the thought of her own Mum no longer being around. They'd been worried for a while when she had a health scare some months back but fortunately it turned out to be just that, a scare, a false alarm. And Hazel was so grateful that it was nothing serious. She wouldn't even dare to think about what her life would be like without her precious Mum.

She found herself thinking that it must be awful for Mr James, Benjamin, to have lost his mother so young. Then she corrected herself again. It was very sad for him but she was not, repeat not, going to fall for another impossibly good looking, vain man and make an idiot of herself like she had with Adam. No way would she ever do that again. She was certain of that. Wasn't she?

Pulling herself together, Hazel resolved to forget about Mr Benjamin James and concentrate on herself, work and paying off the bills for a while. All that romance malarky could wait until somebody sensible came along in a few years' time.

She carefully removed her make-up and moisturised her face, brushed her teeth vigorously and put on a pair of comfy pyjamas then curled up in her bed.

With far too many thoughts rushing around in her head after the evening she'd had, it took her quite a while to eventually get to sleep and, when she did, she kept having dreams about Mr James in a suit of armour fighting off a fire-breathing dragon which, unluckily for the dragon, just happened to look a lot like Rebecca Stevens and appeared to have the same unpleasant demeanour as her too.

Hazel finally abandoned all hope of getting a good night's sleep at half past five in the morning. She got out of bed to do some aerobics to her favourite feel-good songs, to work off some of those calories she'd taken on board the evening before.

Then she had a shower and started getting herself dressed and preparing her packed lunch ready for work. And, of course, she needed to brace herself for Alice's inevitable questioning about how the evening had turned out.

Hazel began to debate how much she should tell Alice about the evening. She didn't want Alice to guess the way Mr James, Benjamin, was making her feel. Or, perhaps to be even more accurate, she tried to work out how she could hide, from Alice, the way Mr James was making her feel, even if feeling the way she did was very, very much against her better judgement.

CHAPTER TEN

Alice Learns the Juicy Details

Sure enough, when Hazel arrived at work, she discovered that Alice was already waiting in the office, cups of coffee at the ready, in eager anticipation of learning all the exciting and, as Alice called them, 'the juicy details' of her evening out with the mysterious Mr James.

Hazel had to go through absolutely everything that had happened from the time she left Alice at work, beginning with the shopping trip to the Outlet.

Alice said she was desperate to see the outfit she had purchased and, fortunately for Hazel, she had remembered to take photographs on her phone of the dress, the coat, the bag and the shoes, even if it had been earlier that morning when she was no longer wearing them.

"Oh, wow, that dress is so pretty," Alice declared. "And I love the shoes and the bag too. You must have looked so beautiful."

"Thank you, Alice. I know I was really lucky to find them," agreed Hazel, "Though I could never have managed to sort everything out in time without that helpful Shop Assistant, I must go back one evening to say thank you to her."

"That would be very thoughtful," Alice agreed. "So, come on then, tell me what happened when the mysterious Mr James picked you up? How was he dressed, I bet he looked really dashing!"

"Oh, yeah, like you'd expect, more snappily dressed even than usual," Hazel explained. "An extremely smart suit, red and grey striped tie, very shiny black leather shoes and a ridiculously expensive cologne, of course."

She explained that Mr James collected her from the lobby of the flats at 7 as promised and drove her over to the Cygnets Restaurant.

"Oh, is his car *very* flashy?" asked Alice.

"Of course, ridiculously flashy," grinned Hazel.

"I knew it would be!"

"Yeah, it's a fancy green BMW. An 8 series Gran Coupe, in Sanremo Green Metallic with black full merino leather interior to be precise. It does 0-62 miles per hour in 3.9 seconds. And it has a fuel consumption of 26.2 miles per gallon," Hazel informed Alice.

"Did he tell you that and you remembered it all?" asked Alice, looking very impressed at her for recalling all the details.

"No," Hazel laughed. "He told me the first bit, about it being an 8 Series Gran Coupe and I just said it was a nice colour."

"Ha ha ha, good on you, girl," replied Alice.

"Yeah, I know all the rest of the spec because my little brother likes all those fancy cars and constantly jabbers on about them, shoving pictures of them into my face, when I see him," Hazel informed her.

"Oh, right, so a typical little brother! And then mysterious Mr James took you to the Cygnets Restaurant?"

"Yes, that's right. And you were totally correct, of course, Alice. It does look very swanky from the outside. You can tell it's a very expensive restaurant just by looking at it," Hazel confirmed.

"And was the food as good as they say?" asked Alice.

Hazel agreed that the food was fabulous, though she could never have imagined herself eating snails and rare steak like Rebecca did.

"Yeuch," exclaimed Alice, wrinkling her nose in disgust. "That sounds about right for her, from what I've heard of her. Anyway, what happened after you left the restaurant? That's the juicy details I'm looking for," she laughed.

Hazel told Alice how Mr James had taken her home and that he had come running back to her to collect the pendant. "He said it had belonged to his late Mum and he'd bought it with his first bonus at work," she clarified.

"Oh, poor guy," Alice exclaimed, "He's awfully young to have lost his Mum."

"Yeah, I know, it must be dreadful for him," Hazel said.

"It must be," Alice agreed. "So was it very beautiful, this pendant?" she asked.

Hazel described the necklace, 18 carat gold, a huge pear-shaped emerald and surrounded by diamonds. She even ended up drawing a picture of it at about its actual size so Alice could really appreciate how dazzling it truly was.

"Crikey, that must be worth a small fortune!" Alice exclaimed. "He must have got quite a bonus to be able to buy that for his Mum, it's so sad that she evidently didn't get to keep it for long."

"Yeah, I know," agreed Hazel. "It is sad. Really sad." She swallowed, trying to dampen down all those annoying emotions that talking about Mr James caused her to feel.

"Anyway," she said, changing the subject, "I must get on with my work today, I've got loads to do and there are a couple of details of these contracts that I need to speak to you about."

"Oh yes, we really must crack on with work, we can't spend all day talking about your dinner date at an exclusive restaurant with an extremely handsome man named Mr Benjamin James. I mean who wants to sit and talk about that all day?" chuckled Alice.

Hazel laughed, despite herself, then they settled down to that companionable silence again, with Alice managing to contain herself and only ask a couple of more questions about the evening, which Hazel was very grateful for. She didn't know how she would answer if Alice questioned her too closely about how she felt about Mr James after the evening they'd spent together.

To stop any further interrogation as they packed up to go home, Hazel told Alice she was so pleased with the outfit that she had decided to go that evening after work to say thank you to the Shop Assistant.

She managed to escape from Alice without too much difficulty at 5 o'clock and, as she was standing outside the shop in the Outlet that had sold her the items, Hazel was happy to see, almost immediately, the Sales Assistant who'd helped her the previous evening.

The Assistant was pleased to see Hazel, delighted with her praise and also very glad to hear that they had had a lovely evening at the Cygnets Restaurant and that the other people she was dining with had really admired her outfit.

The Shop Assistant requested a good review on the company website so Hazel made sure to write that feedback on as soon as she got home, giving the service 5 stars and leaving a comment about how helpful Julie, the Shop Assistant who served her, had been.

CHAPTER ELEVEN

Mr James Again

A few days after they'd gone to dinner, the mysterious Mr James appeared at Hazel's office door with that pearly white, toothy grin on his face again. The one that made his eyes twinkle in that annoyingly attractive way.

He stepped into the office and said he was delighted to tell her that the evening had been a roaring success. They had won the contract they were negotiating, an important one for the company, and he was convinced it was partly due to her as she was so lovely and the clients and their wives all said the same thing. And, even better, his relationship with Mr Stevens was still cordial and he'd managed to stop Rebecca from getting her claws into him, so it was a truly excellent result all round.

Then, he smiled at Hazel and said something else to her, looking at her in what appeared to her to be an encouraging manner, but she just couldn't make out the words he'd spoken because there was a loud screeching sound and red flashing lights. They both looked up to the ceiling, realising the fire alarms were going off.

This was followed, as always, by those brief moments when everyone in the offices looks at everyone else, wondering if it's a false alarm and if the ear-shattering ringing and flashing lights will stop soon. Alice had been on the coffee run again, she'd just returned from there and was standing in the doorway holding two cups full of hot coffee.

The next thing that happened, though, was that the sprinklers went off, showering everyone in cold water and dripping into the already full coffee cups Alice was holding.

At that point they had no choice but to evacuate the building. Alice put the cups on the nearest desk and the three of them hurriedly left the office. Hazel followed Alice to the stairs. All the people on the second floor were running about in the corridors, with some trying to remember where the fire exits were, while Hazel could see others moving around outside, many of them clearly trying to recall which assembly point in the car park they should go to.

Somewhere in the rush of leaving the building, everyone gathering in their designated assembly points in the car park, the mutterings of annoyance from some that it would be another drill or false alarm and the appropriate head counts being carried out, Hazel lost sight of Mr James. The last time she remembered seeing him, he was heading upstairs, she guessed to the top floor where he worked, rather than down the stairs to leave the building as he ought to have done.

Even when they were all finally given permission by the Fire Officer to go back into their offices, after he was reassured it was a false alarm, she still couldn't see any sign of Mr James.

She knew he had to be safe, because the Fire Officer was content that everyone was accounted for, but very unhappy that it took so long to evacuate the building and that people didn't know their nominated fire exits and assembly points. Hazel could hear him mumbling under his breath that they needed bigger notices in the offices and that there would be more fire drills until they got this right and everyone left in the required time.

Hazel hoped that mysterious Mr James would come back again to see her and say whatever it was he was trying to say to her when the alarms went off. And, of course, she dreamed it would be what she wanted to hear: something about how he felt about her or asking her to go on another dinner date with him.

However, to her dismay, he didn't come back that day, nor in the following couple of days. She heard nothing from him or about him, during that time, except Alice discovered via the office grapevine that Mr James had gone upstairs during the fire to doublecheck that everyone on his floor got out safely, including Mr Stevens as he was an older man and office rumour had it that he was not in the best of health.

For several days afterwards, Hazel jumped and, despite her protestations to Alice of not being interested at all in the mysterious Mr James, she looked up expectantly every time a figure went past in the corridor or someone came to their office door.

As the Fire Officer had promised, new and bigger notices went up in all the offices and emails went round reminding everyone of their nearest fire exit and assembly point and stressing the importance of every member of staff being aware of them. There was even another fire drill on the Friday morning but Hazel still couldn't see Mr James anywhere in the crowds.

She soon grew to the stage where she desperately tried to shut down Alice's enquiries as to what had happened between them and what Mr James had been saying to her when the alarms went off. Hazel made every effort to pretend that she was not interested, in the slightest bit, in any news that Alice's questioning of her many contacts in the building might discover about Mr Benjamin James. But Alice clearly didn't believe her and kept trying to find out what had happened to him.

After about ten days or so, Alice's speaking to the people she knew, who worked on the higher floors, paid off and she found out that Mr James had been sent over to Canada to represent the firm, having to stand in at the last moment when another more senior staff member was unexpectedly taken ill with appendicitis. The word was that Mr James would be away in Canada for a couple of months and he would only be due to return home to this country shortly before Christmas.

Hazel claimed to Alice that she wasn't interested in the news about mysterious Mr Benjamin James but, in reality, she just couldn't shake that feeling of being abandoned. She tried not to let it show but Alice guessed anyway and kept trying to reassure her, stating she was absolutely certain that Mr James would be back to see her when he returned from Canada in a few weeks' time.

Hazel was pretty convinced that he wouldn't. If he'd really wanted to find her, she fully believed he would have been able to at least find her number, via the switchboard, and give her a call from the company offices in Canada.

It didn't appear to her that, whatever it was he was trying to say to her when the alarms went off, could have been very important. And she was quite sad about that, although she tried to hide it, even from herself, trying desperately to convince herself that she was better off without the mysterious Mr James or indeed any ridiculously good-looking man who would only leave her heartbroken.

CHAPTER TWELVE

The Flood

Just a couple of weeks after Mr James went away to Canada, the offices on the second floor suffered an electrical fire which damaged water pipes and caused a huge flood.

No one was hurt because it happened over the weekend and, as luck would have it, the flood water extinguished the fire but several of the office ceilings came crashing down and the water caused major damage to many of the walls and carpets and much of the furniture and office equipment.

The flooding was spotted by a Security Officer in time to prevent damage to other floors in the building but it still caused huge disruption for the company and especially for the occupants of the second floor.

The ladies' bathroom, where the fire started in the false ceiling, was burnt out, while Hazel and Alice's office and many other rooms, including the staff dining room, suffered serious water damage.

The affected rooms were expected to be out of action for about two to three months, while the repairs were completed and the offices were redecorated.

Fire investigation officers concluded that the previous 'false alarm' from the fire alarm was in fact caused by an electrical fault, in wiring concealed in the false ceiling of the ladies' bathroom. The electrical wires reignited, causing a significant fire and this, in turn, caused damage to the fabric of the building including some water pipes, resulting in a major flood.

It was unbelievably fortunate, the Fire Officer told everyone, that the flooding put the fire out, or the whole building could have gone up and, even more lucky, that the Security Officer spotted the water running, or the other lower floors and the basement would have been badly damaged rather than just the second floor. All in all, he said, things could have been a whole lot worse than they were.

However, it was quite clear that it was going to take some time to fix everything as they had to locate the faults in the electrics, repair and make safe the damaged wiring and reinstall new water pipes then totally refurbish and redecorate all the affected rooms. Most of the furniture, the computing equipment, visual display boards and the plasterboard walls had been ruined and needed to be replaced.

Hazel, Alice and their other colleagues from the second floor were forced to rescue whatever they could from their own offices and cram themselves into different rooms, wherever space could be found for them. Some unlucky people even ended up in the dark and dingy basement, where all the musty old files were stored, but Hazel and Alice were fortunate enough to at least be moved to offices next door to each other on the third floor so they could still see each other occasionally.

They managed to find time to chat now and then, when using the photocopier or on their breaks at the coffee machine. But, naturally, being jammed into the corner of someone else's office meant it wasn't as easy for them to communicate with each other as it was when they were sharing their own space. It was very hard to keep their conversations private, away from the listening ears of the other staff on the third floor. And, of course, there wasn't even the staff dining room available for them to meet up on their lunch breaks, as that too was on the second floor and had been badly damaged in the flood, needing some pretty major repairs itself.

Hazel found the situation especially difficult because, apart from her frequent phone calls home to her Mum, her social life in the city pretty much revolved around her chats with Alice and, very occasionally, nipping out for lunch to a sandwich shop or after work for a quick meal together. It was much more difficult to arrange these occasions on the spur of the moment when they no longer shared an office and everyone else could hear what they were talking about. And also Alice couldn't easily engage Hazel in casual conversation and work out when she was in need of a bit of a boost to her mood or desperate for a little social interaction.

They carried on like this for several weeks. Working in their different borrowed office spaces next door to each other on the third floor, they would do their best to try to snatch moments together, when they could manage to, and time their coffee breaks at the same hour. But that wasn't always easy because they had to work around the timetables of other staff, in the offices they were sharing, and take second place to the existing occupants and their previously agreed routines.

As time moved on, Alice became very adept at finding an excuse to pop into the office next door to her to ask Hazel something work-related. Then, judging how well she was coping on her own, Alice would sometimes drop a note onto her desk on some pretext, asking her to meet for coffee after work or suggesting going out to one of the sandwich shops on a lunchtime. She usually offered to buy something for Hazel too, on these occasions, as she knew just how tight her finances were, after Adam leaving her so badly in debt. Hazel grew to appreciate even more how lucky she was to have such a good friend as Alice.

Hazel heard nothing about the mysterious Mr Benjamin James either directly or via Alice, during these weeks, and she tried her very hardest to forget about him.

But she couldn't do anything to prevent those recurring dreams that she still had of the mysterious Mr James fighting off the dragon, Rebecca, and those even worse ones where, with a ridiculously white smile and sparkling brown eyes, he ran across the lobby of the flats to take her in his arms and declare his undying love for her.

During the day she squashed away any thoughts of Mr James deep inside her but it was a much harder job to stop him from emerging in her dreams, and those dreams began to increase in frequency as she knew that he was due back in this country any day now.

Hazel couldn't help but hope, just a tiny bit, that he would come to find her even if she told herself she was being ridiculous to just so much as think that.

And of course, she had to keep reminding herself that she was off men for good, or for the foreseeable future at least, so she shouldn't even be interested in what Mr Benjamin James might or might not do when he came back from Canada. But those dreams of men in shining suits and dragons still kept coming back when she was asleep and she could do absolutely nothing to stop them.

CHAPTER THIRTEEN

Out for Lunch

One Saturday, with just three weeks to go before Christmas, Hazel was invited out to a nice late afternoon meal, at a well-known family friendly café in the city, with Alice, her husband and their kids.

The café, Luigi's, had been in the city for a very long time and thrived on family groups bringing their children along. It served, all throughout the day, wonderful tea and coffee along with lovely sandwiches and pastries while providing kids meals and drinks, friendly fully childcare trained staff and plenty of toys for the children too, including an enclosed outdoor playground, ball pool and lots of art equipment for different ages. They even had weekly competitions where the best picture, as chosen by customers, would win a free child's meal. All in all, it was perfect for both children and parents and that was the secret of its success.

The plan for them meeting up that Saturday was to exchange Christmas presents early and enjoy a proper catch-up, because Alice and Hazel could hardly speak to each other at work and they wouldn't be seeing one another at all for some time. The following Friday was the start of the company's traditional four week long holiday break and Hazel would be going back to her family home for those few weeks.

Hazel, Alice and Alice's husband, Rick, shared an informal meal of coffee, sandwiches and pastries, that late afternoon, while the children ran around and had fun in the playground, coming back to their own little table for food and drinks and to check in with the adults when they wanted to. That first hour or so was the most enjoyable time Hazel had had in a very long while.

Alice's husband was full of life and very amusing, a real comic who always cheered Hazel up and the children were as delightful as ever. They had insisted on buying their own presents for Hazel and, during the meal, gave her a meticulously wrapped gift from each of them, which they pleaded with her to open that day. She finally agreed and, to the children's obvious delight, she tore off the wrapping paper, with great ceremony, to reveal a pink fluffy rabbit and a bottle of lavender bath crystals. She promised to treasure their gifts, and indeed she would, because it was clear the children had chosen those things especially for her and that brought a tear or two to her eye.

She was having a completely delightful time of it until, whilst popping across to the ladies' bathroom, Hazel was forced to make a detour around the far side of the cafe. In the middle of the room were a large family group, which appeared to her to consist of three or four grandparents, quite a few parents and a large number of children and grandchildren. They were arranging seating and highchairs around several tables for the adults and their accompanying children, who ranged in age from a couple of babies and toddlers up to 12 or 13 or so years of age. Hazel decided to go the long way round to avoid getting in their way while they settled everyone down.

As she walked right around the outside of the room to allow the family group to sort themselves out, a movement to the right caught her eye, perhaps because there was some familiarity in it. She glanced towards a couple sitting close together in a nearby booth, seated with their backs against the wall.

As she looked across at the two of them, Hazel was absolutely horrified to realise that the man was Mr James, sometimes known as Benjamin or even, on occasion, *my* Benjamin. He was smiling his impossibly white smile, his brown eyes were twinkling, as much as they always did, and he was as snappily dressed as ever, this time with a narrow bright green tie to go with a stylish grey three-piece suit and crisp white shirt.

And he was sharing a table with, indeed sitting very, very close beside and cosying up to, a slim girl with long blonde wavy hair. She was wearing a short grey sparkly lurex dress and looked to Hazel to be a couple of years younger than Mr James. They clearly only had eyes for each other and were completely oblivious to anything else going on around them, including Hazel standing staring at them just a few yards away.

To make matters even worse, this girl – a tall willowy blonde (aren't they always, thought Hazel) - was clearly wearing his mother's pendant around her neck. The beautiful, precious emerald and diamond necklace that Mr James, Benjamin, had loaned her on the special evening that they'd gone out to dinner, was sitting there in the café glistening around the neck of another girl!

Hazel was devastated and tears sprung to her eyes as she put her hand up to her mouth to stifle her sobs.

The couple were involved in a very close conversation, holding hands, with eyes only for each other. Mr James had one hand propped up under his chin, as he gazed at the girl, taking in every word she was saying, while his other hand held on tight to hers. They never noticed Hazel at all as she stood rooted to the spot, watching them in horror for what seemed to her like an eternity.

Then, with her face burning, hand still over her mouth to mute her sobbing, she turned away and dashed to the bathroom to keep wiping away the constant stream of tears that just kept welling back up into her eyes again.

She felt so completely betrayed.

Hazel knew it made no real sense to feel the way she did. Logically, she was perfectly aware of the fact that, all she and Mr James had shared, was a handful of interactions and one evening out, lovely as it had been. After that he'd disappeared to Canada for several weeks, without so much as a word. Well, apart from when they were interrupted by the fire alarm, of course, but he didn't come back to tell her whatever he was trying to say then so it mustn't have been that important. She had absolutely nothing else to base her feelings on.

She knew all of that. But knowing it was totally illogical to feel the way she did, still didn't stop it from hurting her so badly nor stop her from feeling as if she'd been totally betrayed by him.

Hazel spent quite a few minutes trying to regain some composure. Eventually, using face powder and concealer from her bag to disguise her blotchy face from them, she pulled herself together enough to go back in and speak to Alice and her family. She knew that they would come looking for her soon if she didn't return anyway.

She tried her best to join in the rest of the conversation, wished Alice, Rick and their delightful children a very happy Christmas and promised faithfully to keep the gifts Alice had bought her wrapped up until Christmas Day. But, as soon as she could decently do so, she made her excuses to the family, saying she was very tired, really in need of the Christmas break and left to go home early.

Back in her flat, Hazel threw off her clothes, dragged on her favourite warm pyjamas and the cuddly pink dressing gown that her Mum had bought her and lay down on the bed, sobbing into her pillow.

She should have just known that bloody Mr Benjamin James was too good to be true, she really should have known.

When she'd been trying to think logically over the past few weeks, she didn't honestly believe he would come back to see her when he returned from Canada.

However, she still couldn't stop a tiny spark of hope from rising up now and again – even if she kept damping it down and wouldn't let it grow to anything more than that tiny spark. Except, of course, in the dreams she kept having of knights in shining suits defending themselves against dragons named Rebecca and rushing to declare their undying love for her.

Well, at least she'd still had that tiny spark of hope until she saw bloody Mr Benjamin James snuggling up with that blonde girl in the café. Now it had been extinguished completely and quite brutally.

And, to make Hazel feel even worse, although that was barely possible, the girl was wearing what she kind of thought of as her pendant. She knew it wasn't really her pendant but equally she didn't expect bloody Mr Benjamin James to be giving away the precious necklace, that meant so much to him and belonged to his mother, to some other girl within days of returning from Canada either.

She knew for certain it had to have been just within a few days of him coming back home. Alice's investigations had managed to find out the approximate date of Mr James' expected arrival back in the UK, via her contacts upstairs on the top floor, and he would only have made it back home a maximum of two or three days ago.

And, of course, it was because he wasn't in a relationship that he had to pretend to Mr Stevens and Rebecca that he had a girlfriend, decide to sit with Hazel in the staff dining room and then invite her out for dinner after Mr Stevens recognised her by her red hair. So, all in all, he could only have known this bloody blonde girl just a few days and he was already giving away his Mum's precious necklace to her, as if it meant absolutely nothing to him. What a cad, he must be!

CHAPTER FOURTEEN

Mr James Returns

On the Tuesday morning, Alice was positively bursting with excitement. When Hazel went to get a coffee from the vending machine, Alice followed her along the corridor and told her that the news on the office grapevine was that Mr James had now returned home, after a very successful trip to Canada.

She told Hazel to look out for him coming by to see her soon. It seemed that he'd been stuck in the office with Mr Stevens all day on the Monday doing a debrief. The word was that they'd barely stopped for lunch as there was so much to discuss. And Alice had found out that they were due to do the same thing that day, Tuesday, too but Mr James was expected to have some free time scheduled later in the week.

Hazel pretended not to be interested in her news and changed the subject away from Mr James' to discussing her arrangements for Christmas instead. She told Alice she was looking forward so much to going home to her family for the holidays and was concentrating on that, instead of thinking about Mr James. Alice looked surprised but went along with it, albeit a little reluctantly, and listened intently to Hazel's plans for Christmas with the family, saying how pleased she was that Hazel was obviously going to have a great time meeting up with all of her family and friends in her village.

Hazel thought she'd got away with it with Alice until, as they were parting company, Alice said to her, "Don't worry, I have it on good authority that he has been really busy in Canada and Mr Stevens has had him pinned down in the office since he got back. I'm almost certain, judging by the way he was making eyes at you on the day when we were flooded out, that he does like you and he will come back to see you. And if he doesn't, he's a complete idiot anyway and you're better off without him."

Hazel just nodded and said, "Thanks." She simply couldn't bear to admit to Alice that she'd seen Mr James with some blonde girl in the café. She knew talking about it all would upset her so much and she didn't want to start sobbing and make a fool of herself in front of Alice. So she decided it was safer to just go along with Alice's assumption that she was annoyed with Mr James for not getting in touch with her while he was away in Canada or since he came back.

On the Wednesday evening, Mr Benjamin James, with an apologetic smile on his face, put his head around the door of Hazel's temporary new office to try to catch her just as she was leaving for home. The other two occupants of that office and Alice had all gone home a little early that day but Hazel had important work to finish and couldn't leave until her proper finishing time.

"Oh, I've found you, Red," Mr James said. "Sorry I've been a while in coming to see you. This is the first chance I've had. I haven't been back in this country very long and I've just been busy, for the past couple of days, updating Mr Stevens with all the news from Canada and the new contract, which seems to be going swimmingly."

"Oh, that's good," said Hazel flatly, deliberately looking away from him.

"And talking of swimming," added Mr James, "I hear there was a bit of a flood on the second floor and some of the offices are still being repaired, which I'm guessing is why you've been placed in the corner of this office here on the third floor."

"Yeah, that's right," said Hazel, turning her back on him and picking up her bag.

"It must have been pretty bad, judging by how long everything is taking to fix. But the good news is, we're expecting everything will be back to normal after the Christmas break," he said brightly, clearly trying to keep the conversation going and work out why Hazel wasn't responding to him with the enthusiasm he'd expected.

"Yeah, that's good," Hazel replied.

Then she told him decisively that she had somewhere else to go that evening so regrettably she couldn't stay and chat.

To her surprise, he looked genuinely disappointed and explained, "I honestly did try to call you while I was away in Canada but the switchboard couldn't put me through because your extension number wasn't working. Now I know why. You were moved out of your office because of the flood and the phone lines were down. But I'm here now and, honestly, I searched this whole building until I spotted you. I'd recognise you anywhere, Red."

"Sorry," she said, "I have to go now," and she swung her heavy black holdall onto her shoulder, marched straight past him out of the door and left him staring after her.

She was positively fuming. How dare he pretend that he had simply not been able to contact her when, in reality, he was dallying with a blonde girl behind her back? Did he take her for a complete idiot?

Well, technically, she knew 'behind her back' didn't really describe it. But he clearly hadn't exactly been heartbroken at not being able to make contact with Hazel and had managed to find another girl to console him easily enough, and just within days of coming back from Canada too, hadn't he? He sure as all heck hadn't wasted much time, had he?

And, as if things weren't already bad enough, he'd even given that girl, someone he'd known only five minutes, the precious pendant which belonged to his mother. She'd thought, as the necklace meant so much to him and he trusted her enough to lend it to her to wear for their evening out, that she must mean something special to him too. What an idiot she felt!

CHAPTER FIFTEEN

Hazel Goes Home

Mr Benjamin James didn't come by her office again, which was just as well as Hazel would definitely have given him a piece of her mind, and, at the end of the week, the company closed for the Christmas break.

It was a company tradition that they closed for four weeks over Christmas. Those of a charitable nature said it was because it was important to the company that their staff had a good work-life balance; the less charitable ones muttered something about the company being too mean to pay the bill for the offices to be heated during the coldest time of the year.

Whatever the reason, Hazel was very grateful for not having to go to work over the seasonal holidays and extremely pleased to be going home to rejoin her family for Christmas. She really missed them when she was working away in the city but she had no choice because she needed this well-paid job to enable her to pay off the debts Adam had left her in.

She calculated that, if she stayed in her current job another 18 months and kept her spending to the bare minimum, she could pay off the loan a little earlier than originally planned and she would be debt free at last. Then she could begin to think about a proper life of her own again.

At that time, she would decide whether it was a better idea for her to return home and find work in her own village, or perhaps in the nearby town, or whether she should stay and try to develop some sort of social life in the city where she was living. It really hampered the opportunity to make new friends when she couldn't afford to go out socialising and even struggled to return the favour if someone so much as bought her a coffee.

Hazel had never told her Mum and Dad the full extent of the debts that Adam had left her in. She knew for a fact that they would have insisted on paying it all off for her, if she told them how bad it was, but she didn't want them to pay for her mistakes, especially since her Mum had warned her repeatedly about him during their relationship.

Once or twice, during the time her and Adam were together, her Mum had even questioned Hazel why she always had to pay for everything and asked when he was going to take some of that responsibility? But Hazel, young and in love, believed every single excuse Adam made. She knew now that she would never be silly enough to make the same mistake again.

After taking debt management advice from the Citizens Advice Bureau, Hazel had combined all of the loans into one larger loan with a single payment per month, so she knew the exact amount she needed to earn to cover it. Then she found work in the city, because the jobs were better paid there than nearer home, pretending to her Mum and Dad that she had decided it was time to spread her wings. They helped her find her little flat at a fairly reasonable rent, somewhere relatively safe and comfortable where there were lots of people about.

When she finally started the job and moved into the flat, Hazel sat down and worked out the amount she would need to spend on rent, utilities and paying off the debt and precisely how much she would have left to spend on food and any clothing she might need and she stuck to it rigidly. She had no choice. There was just no other way to manage. But she found it so difficult being on her own without her family around her, particularly when she couldn't admit to them how lonely she felt being away from them, since she'd told them it was her idea to jump out on her own into the big wide world.

She was so grateful to be able to spend time with the family at Christmas, she really didn't think she could bear the idea of being on her own during those special holidays.

When the Friday came, the company stopped work at lunchtime. Alice and Hazel hugged warmly and wished each other a very merry Christmas. Hazel went back to the flat, grabbed the suitcase she had packed and walked to the bus station to catch the first of the two buses she needed to travel on to get home.

It took Hazel about two hours of travelling on the coaches but, thankfully, her Dad and little brother, Tommy, were already waiting at the station ready for her when she got there. She threw her suitcase in the car boot – she travelled fairly light as most of her favourite clothes were still in her wardrobe at home – and hopped into the back of the car because her little brother was hogging the front seat as usual.

All the way home, her brother chattered away to her, telling her what he'd been up to while she'd been away, what he'd been doing at school and, of course, all the details he'd been learning about the latest cars he wanted to buy when he was a grown up.

Hazel briefly wondered what he'd say if he found out that she'd been driven around in a Sanremo Green BMW Series 8 Gran Coupe with black full merino leather interior. She decided it was best not to say anything to him or he'd be asking her too many questions and she knew how sad that would make her feel.

Just thinking about Mr Benjamin James and his shiny green Beamer and his perfect white smile, not to mention his twinkling brown eyes and his impeccably tailored suits and him meeting willowy blondes in cafés, made her so sad, talking about him would be simply unbearable, so Hazel carefully steered her thoughts away from him.

While they were travelling, her Dad whistled cheerily to the music on the car radio and told her how much he missed her and how much he was looking forward to having the family back together again for the holidays. Hazel did say to him how lovely it was for her to be home with them for the holidays too, but she knew she had to try not to overdo it, in case he picked up that she was a bit too keen to be home, for someone who claimed she wanted to strike out on her own and spread her wings.

She loved looking out of the car window and watching the familiar places go by, as they travelled along roads which became more and more rural with more and more sheep in the fields around them, as they got close to home. After driving from the station for about 15 minutes, they turned into their village. They drove past the small Primary School that Hazel and her brother had attended, the Library where her Mum worked, the crossroads next to the tiny church with its tall crooked bell tower that signalled they were so nearly home. Then finally they passed by the houses of a couple of neighbours and reached the dormer bungalow where Hazel grew up, surrounded by lots of family and friends in their little village. Her Dad pulled up in front of the garage at the side of the bungalow and took the suitcase out from the car boot, carrying it inside for her.

Hazel opened the little front gate, the way she used to do when she came back from school, or when she'd been out with her schoolfriends as a teenager. It was a silly thing but she really missed the sound of the latch, as she opened it inwards then left it to automatically swing shut behind her, and she couldn't wait to hear it again. She ran up the front path, past the old apple tree in the lawn and up the few steps to the red front door and began to feel she was properly home at last.

When she finally got into the house, Hazel felt that huge sense of relief flow over her at finally being in what she still thought of as her own home. She wasn't in the least bit surprised to see lots of assorted glass jars of carefully labelled jam and chutney on the shelves in her Mum's cosy, warm kitchen with its golden oak cupboards and farmhouse kitchen table with its lace tablecloth and willow pattern placemats in the centre.

Her mother had obviously been busy, the same as she always was in the run-up to Christmas, making a variety of preserves from the glut of fruit and vegetables – apples, blackcurrants, tomatoes, onions, peppers and many other things - that the greenhouse and garden provided in the autumn. Hazel could see jars of chutney - green tomato, red tomato and rhubarb and onion - along with plum, apple and blackberry, strawberry and blackcurrant jam. They positively gleamed in the light and she knew they would all taste absolutely delicious.

Her lovely Mum was in the kitchen in the middle of baking and, when she saw Hazel standing in the doorway, she wiped the flour from her hands onto her apron then ran to embrace her in a huge warm hug.

Hazel felt herself just completely crumble once she was in the safety of her Mum's arms.

Mum made light of it, pretending to Dad and her little brother that Hazel was just grateful to be home and how lovely it was that she'd missed them all so much, but her Mum knew there was more to it than that and whispered that they'd talk later.

Hazel nodded gratefully while her Mum distracted them all, with cakes and tea and chatting about what preserves she'd been making and all the events in the village she was planning for them to attend.

She reminded Hazel of the friends and family who were so looking forward to her visiting them while she was home, including Great Auntie Kathleen who'd demanded to be first in the queue, their neighbours Diane and Keith who were coming for Christmas dinner, Hazel's best friend Natalie, who couldn't wait to see her and had some special news for her, and many others.

Her Mum worked for a couple of days a week in the local Library and volunteered for another two days at the nearby Primary School, which Hazel and her brother had both attended previously. Her brother was now in his first year at Secondary School, in the nearby town, and her Mum spent her time at the Primary School, listening to the children read and helping out on school trips.

The school was already winding down for the Christmas holidays and the Library only opened two days a week in the two weeks before Christmas anyway, meaning Hazel's Mum only covered one day in the week there. Mum had had lots of free time on her hands and she had spent it decorating the Christmas cakes that she made weeks ago and baking ginger biscuits, as well as cooking up all the preserves that Hazel had just spotted, the Christmas puddings already having been made about two months ago, as was the tradition.

Some of the produce would go as prizes to the local community centre fair, some went to family and friends as presents and the rest they shared, as a family with Christmas dinner, or as accompaniments to the many meals of leftovers that they would enjoy with whichever friends or relatives popped by.

Hazel's Dad, Bill, had worked for many years as a manager in the pharmaceutical industry but he had long since taken early retirement on a tidy pension.

He now spent his time playing golf and pottering about in the garden, making sure there was a good supply of fruit and vegetables for Mum's home-made sauces, chutneys and jams, as well as apples from the old apple tree in the front garden for apple sauce and her glorious cinnamon scented apple pies, which were Hazel's absolute favourite of all the baking her Mum did. No one else could ever make apple pies as good as her Mum's.

Of course, Hazel had never told her Mum and Dad the true extent of the debt Adam had left her in.

While she was still trying to get over the shock of what he'd done to her, her Mum had found a couple of opened letters, Hazel had accidentally left lying around, demanding money and cleared them off for her. There were so many of those letters, it was hard to keep track of them all and she felt awful that her Mum had found even those ones. Her Mum had no idea how many more there were.

And, of course, her Mum and the rest of the family had no clues as to the real reason why Hazel was working in the city, or how much she missed her family and wished she was back living with them.

She could never tell her the truth, or her Mum would insist that she came to live back at home and that they paid her debts off, which Hazel didn't think was fair. She felt she was to blame for allowing Adam to get away with it and, of course, her Mum had warned her several times about him and how he always persuaded her to pay for everything and she should have listened to her Mum instead of taking notice of Adam's many excuses. Hazel was determined she would never make the same mistake again.

But at least she was home for Christmas and intending to make the most of it, getting involved in village events and visiting all her friends and relatives, before she had to go back to her little flat in the city and set her nose to the grindstone again to pay off the debts Adam had run up in her name.

CHAPTER SIXTEEN

Christmas in the Village

With two full weeks still to go until Christmas Day itself, Hazel as always would become involved, along with her Mum and Dad, in the social life of their village. They would be spending their time visiting all the relatives and friends, who were so eager to see Hazel now she was home, as well as attending Christmas parties and helping to organise and take part in the Christmas fair at the community centre.

When she finally found a moment away from her husband and son on Hazel's first day home, her Mum tackled her about the tears when she arrived back and Hazel was forced to confess the whole sorry story of mysterious Mr James, as Alice had named him.

Hazel described to her Mum how this guy, she didn't even know, appeared in front of her one day in the staff dining room and sat down opposite her. She explained that he asked her to talk to him and pretend to be his girlfriend to stop the boss, Mr Stevens, from trying to match him up with his daughter, Rebecca. But Mr Stevens had recognised her by that long red hair of hers, so this man, who Alice dubbed 'the mysterious Mr James', ended up having to come to her office to persuade her to go to dinner at a very smart restaurant with Mr Stevens, Rebecca and some of their clients.

She told her mother how she had nothing suitable to wear for dinner at a fancy restaurant like that, so this man, Mr James, had given her money for an outfit and she'd gone to the Outlet shopping centre and managed to buy a beautiful dress and jacket.

And, when he'd picked her up from her flat, Mr James had even given her the precious 18 carat gold, emerald and diamond pendant, belonging to his late mother, to wear. She explained how they'd had such a lovely evening at the Cygnets Restaurant in the Swan Hotel and it turned out that the Cygnets was so swish that even her Mum had heard of it.

"I was terrified they'd ask me to pay my share of the bill and I'd end up doing the washing up for weeks afterwards," she smiled, making her Mum chuckle. "But, of course, Mr Stevens paid for it all with his credit card so that was a huge relief."

Then Hazel recounted the story of how the dashing, mysterious Mr James dropped her off outside her flat after dinner and, she'd just reached the lift, when he came sprinting back across the lobby to her. But instead of - and Hazel almost burst out laughing at the cliché when she said it in front of her Mum - the traditional happy ending of 'sweeping her up into his arms and begging her to be his girlfriend', he only came back for, as she put it, 'the flipping pendant'.

"To be fair," her Mum pointed out, "That necklace must mean a lot to him if it belonged to his late mother so, I guess, it must show something about how he felt about you that he allowed you to borrow it for the evening."

"I would have thought so," agreed Hazel, then the tears welled up again.

She explained how Mr James had gone away, without a word, after their lovely evening out. He'd disappeared to Canada on company business for a couple of months, and that the next time she saw him was about a week ago, when she was in Luigi's Family Café, sharing a meal with Alice and her family. Just a couple of days after he came back from Canada, he was there in Luigi's getting extremely cosy with a tall blonde girl and, to make matters worse, that girl was wearing the precious gold and emerald necklace that had belonged to his late mother.

"Oh, my dear, I'm so sorry," Hazel's Mum told her as she hugged her in a warm motherly embrace, while she cried on her Mum's shoulder.

After a few moments of this, her Mum pulled back and wiped Hazel's tears away with a tissue. She declared, "What a louse he is. You're far better off without him, my dear."

"I know," sobbed Hazel.

"Was he awfully good looking?" asked her Mum.

"Terribly," sobbed Hazel.

"And very smartly dressed?"

"Very, very smartly dressed," Hazel confirmed.

"And charming and witty?" queried her Mum.

"Yes, of course," agreed Hazel through her tears.

"They're the worst ones," asserted her Mum, nodding vigorously. "Don't you worry, my dear, you'll get over him and find someone else. He might not be as ridiculously good looking or as smartly dressed or as charming and witty as that Mr Louse … but you'll definitely find someone else."

"I know," wailed Hazel. "But it still hurts so much, Mum."

"I know it hurts really bad, my dear, but you will get over Mr Louse, I promise," replied her Mum. "You make sure that you tell him from me what he is when you see him again, that he's an absolute louse. Now, come on, dry up those tears and let's get along to see Auntie Kathleen and forget all about that dreadful Mr Louse."

"Who?" asked Hazel, responding to her cue perfectly, although her voice wavered perilously.

"Exactly," agreed her Mum with a warm smile and a huge hug,

knowing how much Hazel was still hurting despite trying to put a brave face on it all, and off they went to visit Auntie Kathleen, her Mum's elderly Great Aunt, the first of the friends and relatives on their busy schedule.

In the days that followed, lots of visits were arranged to more of the long-lost friends and relatives that Hazel hadn't seen all year, including her best friend, Natalie, who she'd known since they first went to Primary School together. To her surprise, Natalie introduced her to her new boyfriend, Nick. The last she'd heard, Natalie was single so she wasn't expecting her to introduce a boyfriend at all, although Hazel, of course, was delighted for her.

Nick, it transpired, was an earnest young man who took the role of Natalie's boyfriend very, very seriously and was extremely concerned to find out that Hazel didn't have one of her own.

He kept muttering that they would have to do something about that missing boyfriend and Hazel was desperately afraid that he'd bring someone along, from his workplace, to one of the events she was attending in the village and try to match them up.

Nick worked at the local livery stable and, although Hazel believed that he was a decent enough young man, she personally did not find the idea of being paired up with a young gentleman, with a constant aroma of horse manure around him, particularly appealing. Especially after Mr Benjamin James and his smart three-piece suits and his crisp white shirts and his shiny shoes and his glorious aroma of aftershave.

Oh, darn it, she thought, there I go again. I am not, I repeat not, getting myself involved with a good-looking charmer ever again, even if he does smell as good enough to eat as one of my Mum's apple pies.

And, besides, she reminded herself, he'd gone off to Canada, without so much as a word, and abandoned her for weeks, then he was last seen canoodling with a blonde in the café. He was a louse, she had to remember that – he was an absolute louse. Her Mum had said so and her Mum was always right - but it still hurt her so much.

Of course, she knew, looking at it logically, that it was ridiculous to feel the way she did but, somewhere deep inside her, she had still believed that there was a real connection between her and Mr Benjamin James, or at least she had until she saw him cosying up to that willowy blonde girl in the café.

CHAPTER SEVENTEEN

The Community Centre Fair

As well as visiting all their friends and relatives in the weeks before Christmas, it was another tradition that her family became involved in the community centre fair, in one capacity or another. They'd done it for many years, in fact as long as Hazel could remember.

Hazel's Dad did any minor work needed for the centre such as replacing locks and polishing floors and he also sorted out any equipment they needed for the fair, such as covering buckets in Christmas paper for the tombola stalls and any necessary repairs to the Santa's grotto he'd originally constructed several years ago.

As she had for the past three years, Hazel would take over the role of Santa's elf helper, dressed in black pixie boots, dark green leggings and a lighter green overshirt with a funny little cap with a bell on the top.

Her job was to guide the children in to see Santa in his grotto then steer them back out again in good time, before it all became too much for them and the list of presents they wanted for Christmas got too long for their parents to cope with.

Her Mum meanwhile became Mrs Christmas to take over from Santa (otherwise known as Mr Rowntree, the grocer) when he needed a cigarette break or had partaken of a bit too much sherry and needed to sober up for a while.

Eventually, after what seemed like hours, the grotto was over and done with and the last of the children had left with the final few selection boxes. Hazel helped her Mum's friend, Annie, out on the 'name the reindeer stall' and bought some of the remaining tickets at several other raffle and tombola stalls, winning a Christmas teddy bear, which was wearing a rather fetching bright red Santa outfit, and one of her Mum's Christmas puddings back.

At the end of the evening, Hazel and her Mum helped to count up the takings and store them securely in Mr Rowntree's safe. They'd made over £1000 which would be used to buy toys and treats, for the children who attended the playgroup and afterschool group that ran in the community hall during term time, so it was a very successful fundraising event for such a relatively small community.

After the fair there followed a few more days of parties, visiting friends, eating too many mince pies and, especially important for Hazel, trying to avoid Natalie's boyfriend, in particular when he was in the company of a young guy of about her own age.

Indeed, he seemed to find an endless series of them, tall and short, dark and fair, slim and slightly portly, he found them of all shapes and sizes and, if she was unlucky enough to get close enough to them, every one of them did smell of horse manure as she feared they would.

Hazel much preferred expensive aftershave to that particular aroma but, of course, that thought led her to mysterious Mr James, sharp suits, shiny shoes and bloody willowy blondes in cafés so she tried to avoid it as much as possible.

CHAPTER EIGHTEEN

Mr James Pays a Visit

Finally, the afternoon of Christmas Eve came around and, with it, a bit of a lull in the Christmas parties and visits to and from family and friends.

Hazel and her Mum were having a lovely quiet afternoon, enjoying a nice girly chat while her Dad and little brother were out for a final Christmas Eve walk around the village, popping in to see the couple of friends and relatives they still hadn't managed to visit yet and some of her brother's schoolfriends.

Hazel was helping her mother to put the finishing touches, of icing and coloured sprinkles, to some fairy cakes her Mum had made for their Christmas Eve tea, while a beautiful aromatic apple pie sat cooling on a shelf.

It was another family tradition that they would have afternoon tea, including fresh sandwiches, champagne and orange juice as well as some of her Mum's glorious apple pie. Then they would spend the evening swapping Christmas Eve presents of pyjamas, socks, dressing gowns and bottles of spirits, with hot chocolate and marshmallows for the youngest children, in the small group of close family and friends who were invited to tea.

Suddenly, the peace and quiet of their cosy, all-girls-together afternoon was interrupted when there was a firm knock at the door.

They glanced up at each other, her Mum raised her eyebrows

looking puzzled while Hazel shrugged, neither of them had any idea who it could be. They definitely weren't expecting anyone to call at this time of the day, it was usually later in the afternoon for the close friends and family and Christmas morning when the rest of their relatives and friends would begin calling round again.

When her Mum answered the door, Hazel could just see over her Mum's shoulder and realised that Mr James had turned up at her home. She guessed that it must have been Alice who had given him her address – she always was too much of a soppy romantic for her own, or for that matter, for Hazel's own good was Alice, a lovely lady and a really good friend to Hazel though she was.

"Hello. I've come to see Hazel, if she's in," Mr James explained.

He was dressed down, well for him at least, in a dark suit with his shirt collar open at the neck. To Hazel's great annoyance, he looked even more luscious dressed like that, if it were even possible. She hoped that bloody blonde girl was happy with her prize.

"Who shall I say is calling?" asked her Mum.

"Apparently, I'm known as the mysterious Mr James," he replied.

Hazel now knew, beyond all doubt, that it must have been Alice who he had been speaking to, she was the one who had named him the mysterious Mr James, of course.

He continued, "But my proper first name is Benjamin and I'd like to speak to Hazel, who I believe lives here in this dormer bungalow in this little village, miles from the city. I'm guessing that Hazel is your daughter?"

"She is," said her Mum, standing back to let Mr James step into the kitchen.

"You look such a lot like her, I knew you had to be her Mum," Mr James told her with one of those annoying warm smiles that made his eyes crinkle so attractively at the edges.

Her Mum beamed back at him. "Hazel, there's a young man here for you. He says his name is Benjamin," she announced.

"Could we offer you a cup of tea and a mince pie or something while you're here?" her Mum asked Mr James eagerly, looking up at him from her height of around just 5 feet tall and clearly approving of what she saw.

"That sounds delicious but I'm fine for now, thank you," he explained, "I just need to speak to Hazel. If that's okay with you, Mrs Brookes?"

"It's fine with me and call me Angela," her Mum smiled, taking two steps out of the way so Mr James could see Hazel, who was inching further and further back to the rear of the kitchen, trying to keep away from Mr James' view.

"Hazel, this nice young man here, he says his name is Benjamin, has come to see you," she prompted her again.

"Hello," Hazel said stiffly. "I'm guessing it was Alice who gave you my address. She shouldn't have."

Her Mum glanced across at her in surprise, wondering why her daughter was being so rude to this apparently very nice, and obviously very smartly dressed and polite, young man who'd come to visit her

Then the penny dropped. "Ah, you must be Mr Louse," she announced, with a smile and a wink at Hazel.

"If you say so," replied Mr James, shrugging his shoulders, palms of his hands facing upwards. "I've no idea what I've done to Hazel that is so bad that it would justify me being labelled a louse though. I haven't behaved well but I wouldn't have thought it was bad enough to deserve me being called a louse, of all things."

"They all say that," retorted Hazel.

"They do indeed," nodded her Mum, looking enquiringly at Mr James to hear what his defence would be to the allegations, and Hazel could see she was clearly hoping that he would be able to come up with a suitable excuse. Her Mum was obviously quite taken with the mysterious Mr James.

CHAPTER NINETEEN

The Girl in the Café

Benjamin James obviously decided it would be best to ignore the hostility in Hazel's tone, and the insults being thrown his way, and get on with telling her his reason for turning up at her house that Christmas Eve.

"I've brought you something," he said to her as he took, from the top pocket of his suit jacket, the black velvet bag that she knew contained his mother's emerald and diamond pendant. "I want you to have this," he said, removing the necklace from the bag.

"Did *she* give it back to you?" Hazel blurted out.

Her Mum turned to him to see his response to this remark, Benjamin meanwhile was looking towards Hazel with an expression of what appeared to be genuine hurt mingled with real confusion on his face.

Hazel thought to herself that she should have known the mysterious Mr James would be a bloody good actor when he wanted to be, men like him always were.

"She? Who the heck is 'she'? And did she give me what back? What do you mean? I truly don't understand what you're talking about," Benjamin James frowned and shook his head, looking totally bewildered.

Hazel was absolutely furious that he had the nerve to appear genuinely puzzled, as if he had no idea that, a couple of weeks ago, he'd been canoodling with a blonde girl in the city's most famous family restaurant, Luigi's Café.

"Don't lie to me. I bloody saw you with her!" Hazel exclaimed furiously.

"You saw me with her? I don't understand, you saw me with who?" Mr James asked, shaking his head again, as if to rotate all the pieces of the jigsaw around and force it all to form a picture that made some kind of sense.

"That bloody blonde tart who was all over you in the café. What's the matter, has she given you the brush off so you've come crawling back to me again?" she said angrily.

Judging by the changing expressions on his face, from bewilderment to potential light dawning to some kind of clarity, it looked as if something gradually occurred to Mr James.

Finally, he said, "In Luigi's, the family café in the city? About three weeks ago. In fact, let me think, to be precise on the Saturday around 5 or 6 o'clock?"

"Oh, so you admit it now?" Hazel snapped.

Mr James paused then said slowly, "'Well, I kind of admit it, I guess. 'That bloody blonde tart' as you described her, that's my sister, Tanya. We've been going to that café since we were children. It's one of our favourite places. We used to go there often with our Mum and Dad. And we met up there together on Saturday."

"I don't believe you. Don't you dare lie to me like that! Don't take me for a fool!" Hazel cried out, wiping away her tears.

She was determined not to be taken in again by another impossibly good-looking young man who could charm the birds out of the trees – and, to her utter dismay, appeared to be doing precisely that to her mother.

She couldn't believe her Mum, of all people, was being taken in by this act of innocence by Mr James. Hazel herself was absolutely resolute that she would not be treated like an idiot by another good-looking man. Even if her mother apparently was falling for mysterious Mr James' charms, despite warning her repeatedly throughout her relationship with Adam that he was up to no good.

Mr James, still holding the pendant in his left hand, opened up his jacket and reached into the inside pocket, with his right hand, then pulled out the brown leather wallet that Hazel had seen before when he was giving her the cash to buy her outfit for dinner.

Opening the wallet, he removed about half a dozen photographs. He picked out a dog-eared old one and showed it to Hazel.

Two children smiled out at her. They were sitting on a front doorstep, a little boy of about six or seven with big brown eyes and curly golden-brown hair, and a little girl with blonde, in fact almost white, wavy hair, aged around three or four. The little boy had his arms around the girl, pulling her close while she snuggled up to him.

He explained, "We've always been close, me and my little sister. She works as a veterinary surgeon in York. Some of those Yorkshire farmers can be a bit forthright, even downright rude at times, but, if I were a betting man, I'd be prepared to place a sizeable wager on the fact that this is the first time in her life that my little sister, Tanya, has been called a 'bloody blonde tart', although I suppose I can always ask her if you wish."

Hazel stood there glaring at him, unsure whether to believe him or if she should be becoming even more angry at him for trying to deceive her like that.

"To be fair to her," Mr James continued, "She's a lovely girl, with a terrific sense of humour, and I know she'll find it hilarious to have been described as a 'bloody blonde tart'. But I'll have you know that my little sister is a respectable lady and has been engaged to her boyfriend for around three years now. They're right in the middle of arranging their wedding in June next year. And I'm going to be the best man."

An image fluttered unbidden through Hazel's mind - of Mr James looking ridiculously handsome, all dressed up in a morning suit with a top hat, for a wedding - but she cast it away.

Determined not to be taken for a ride again like she had been with Adam and his endless plausible excuses, Hazel thought about the photo for a while longer. "Oh, well, maybe you do have a sister with blonde hair," she conceded, "But that photo still doesn't prove it was you and your sister that I saw in the café."

Mr James searched through the handful of photos again and picked out another one. This one was obviously of the same little girl but, this time, posing for the camera as a long-legged teenager with shoulder length blonde wavy hair. Hazel had to admit to herself that the girl in this picture could also easily have been the blonde girl she saw in Luigi's café with Mr James.

"Oh, okay," Hazel conceded eventually. "Maybe you're right, maybe that girl was your sister."

"She is," he insisted, showing her a third photo of his sister, who this time looked even more like the blonde girl in the café. But, on this occasion, she had her hair fastened up, was wearing jeans and a checked shirt, still looking unbelievably glamorous while standing in a field with sheep and drystone walls in the background. Beside her stood an older, somewhat ruddy cheeked, man. He appeared to be aged around 30 or so and was dressed in tan corduroy trousers and a cream and orange plaid shirt, presumably, Hazel thought, this photo showed his sister and her fiancé.

"That's Tanya and her fiancé, Peter," Mr James confirmed.

"And, for your information," he added, looking down at the

necklace he was still holding in his hand, "The pendant she was wearing isn't this one. I bought one for her and one for my Mum when I got my first major bonus at work. The chain on Tanya's is a couple of inches shorter and the emerald is a slightly different shape, more of an oval whereas this one is a pear-shape. Though they are pretty similar, of course, both 18 carat gold and surrounded by 12 brilliant cut diamonds. I bought them together for the special ladies in my life to celebrate, to give something back for everything they'd both done for me over the years. I just never expected it would end up being the last ever gift I bought for my Mum."

And this time, she could hear the depth of the emotion, the loss in his voice, even though she could tell he was trying really hard not to let it show. The heart she'd kept carefully frozen, since she'd dumped the feckless Adam, melted just a little bit and this time she didn't try quite so hard to stop it either.

"Okay," Hazel agreed, looking again at the photos, "I believe you about that, I guess. It was your sister you were with when I saw you in the café."

"Yes, it was and thank you for believing me," Mr James said, with deep sincerity. "Tanya and myself hadn't seen each other for a couple of months so we arranged to meet up, as soon as possible, when I got back from Canada. As I said, we're very close, even more so since we lost our Mum. That two months must be the longest we've ever been apart in our lives and, certainly, the longest we've gone in seeing each other since Mum died. Thank you for that, thank you for at least believing me about Tanya. It means a lot to me."

He gave one of his bright, impossibly white, smiles to her Mum whose face lit up. She was obviously quite enchanted by the mysterious Mr James, sometimes known as Benjamin, occasionally even *my* Benjamin which, Hazel had to concede, sounded rather good to her at that moment in time, despite the warning voice in her head telling her not to be such a fool again.

CHAPTER TWENTY

A Gift for Hazel

"Anyway," Mr James said, "Now that we've restored my sister's reputation and established she's not a 'bloody blonde tart', there's something important I came here today to do."

He held out the emerald and diamond pendant to Hazel, in the palm of his hand, resting on its black velvet bag. "There's no one I would rather give this to than you, Red. My Mum made me promise, when she knew she was dying, that I'd give it to the special girl who stole my heart, so someone could enjoy it again, the way it deserves.'

"And there's no one who could ever fit that description better than you do. You are a very special girl, funny, feisty and, even better, you have a kind heart. Oh, and you're very beautiful too."

Hazel's Mum said, "Yes, yes she is."

Mr James continued, "No one else could ever steal my heart the way you have (even though I realise you don't want it, after the way I've treated you, and that's your right, of course). But believe me, no one could possibly ever look more beautiful than you do wearing this pendant. I just know it belongs with you even if, it seems, I sadly don't."

Hazel heard her Mum gasp and felt her heart melt, just a little more, for Mr Benjamin James.

"You see, Red," he continued, "Erm, I'm sorry I mean Hazel, don't I? Your name is Hazel."

Her Mum smiled and Hazel nodded, while Mr James continued, "I know you're not interested in a relationship with me. And I really can't blame you. I honestly didn't mean for it to happen that way but, to all intents and purposes, I used you. I took you out for dinner to charm the clients so we could win the contract and I could keep that awful witch Rebecca at arm's length, then I disappeared for weeks without so much as an explanation."

"Yes, you did," Hazel agreed. "You just walked away and left me without a word, I didn't know where you'd gone and when, or even if, you'd be coming back to see me," she said, reaching up and wiping away a tear. It still hurt her a lot.

Mr James added, "I'm truly sorry, Hazel. Alice told me how much it upset you."

"Yes, it really did," said Hazel. "It upset me so much."

Mr James replied, "I could make a whole lot of excuses, such as going to Canada was a really good career move, the chance of a lifetime, and that I only found out about it with a few hours' notice and that I barely had a free moment while I was out there. And, believe me, all of that is true but it was still unforgiveable of me just to walk away without speaking to you first. I could have and should have made the time to talk to you again, explain what I was doing, where I was going, when I'd be back, after we were interrupted by the fire alarms going off. And I'm so sorry about that."

"When you disappeared, I thought you just didn't care, that the lovely evening we shared together at the Cygnets Restaurant meant nothing to you," Hazel told him. "And then, when I saw you with that girl …"

"I know and I'm really sorry. I honestly did try to ring you, once I was settled in properly and I knew my way around our Canada office, but the switchboard couldn't put the call through to the number they had listed for you. Since I've got back, I've found out about the second floor offices being out of use due to the flood, but I will admit though that I could have done more to find you. I could have found your new extension number, asked around to locate where you were working and find some way to make contact with you. And I should have done. It's unforgivable of me, just to leave you like that for all those weeks, I know that and I am truly, truly sorry."

"Yes, you should be," Hazel replied, still hurting at the way she felt he had just abandoned her, even though she was mightily relieved to find out that the girl in the café was just his sister, Tanya.

Mr James continued, "But there's still no one I would rather give this pendant to. You looked so beautiful that night. The necklace fit you so perfectly and it looked so wonderful with your outfit, you are such a beautiful girl. So, think of it as my way of saying sorry, for the way I treated you, and to say thank you for one of the most memorable and special evenings of my life. Even if I did nearly choke on my mineral water when you told them we met doing aqua aerobics!"

Hazel began laughing through her tears at that last remark and said, "Oops, sorry about that."

Her Mum chuckled and exclaimed, "Hazel, how could you?"

"To be fair, it was pretty funny," Mr James told her Mum.

"Anyway, Hazel, here's your pendant, my special gift for a special girl at Christmas. That is, if you'll accept it," he said, handing the necklace over to her.

She took the pendant from Mr James and held it in her hand, looking down at it. It was a beautiful deep green emerald, expertly cut and surrounded by clear white diamonds so it sparkled away in the overhead lights in her Mum's kitchen. It really was a truly beautiful gift.

And with that, Mr Benjamin James smiled his sparkling smile, first at Hazel, then at her Mum (who positively beamed back at him). He said, "Nice to have met you, Mrs Brookes," and nodded his head to say goodbye and thank you to her Mum as he walked away. He went out of the front door, down the steps and along their front garden path, heading for the pavement outside, presumably towards where he had parked his car.

Hazel stood in her Mum's kitchen, holding tight to the pendant and wordlessly watching him leave.

CHAPTER TWENTY-ONE

The Finale

Then her Mum broke the silence that hung in the air.

"Hazel Brookes," her Mum told her firmly, "If you don't run after that lovely young man and bring him back here, I'll do it myself."

"D-do you think I should?" she asked falteringly.

She was still trying to make some kind of sense of all the information Mr Benjamin James had thrown at her that afternoon.

She now knew the blonde girl in the cafe was his sister and he had definitely said he had tried to contact Hazel while he was away. He'd also said something about how she was beautiful, a special girl and there was no one else he'd rather give his Mum's pendant to. And there was definitely something in there about her stealing his heart. And that just happened to be the same way she knew the mysterious Mr Benjamin James had stolen hers, much as she'd tried to deny it to herself and others, including her Mum and Alice.

"Of course, you should run after him and bring him back here," her Mum said insistently. "He's so handsome! And very polite when I opened the door and spoke to him. And so lovely when he was trying to explain himself to you and you were shouting at him. And it was his sister in the café not a girlfriend and he said you'd stolen his heart and I suspect he's done the same to you. And, of course, he's handsome, did I mention that? He's so very, very handsome."

Hazel laughed and agreed that her Mum had already said that Mr James, Benjamin, was handsome.

"I swear," said her Mum, pointing out of the door where Mr James had just gone, "If you don't run along there after him and snap that young man up, I will. Just please don't tell your Dad I said so!"

Hazel smiled, briefly hugged her Mum then handed her the pendant for safe keeping, "Hold onto this for me, Mum," she said then dashed out of the door and into the street, looking left and right, wondering where Mr James had parked his car.

Then she spotted the shiny, green Beamer on the opposite side of the road, Mr Benjamin James' **BMW 8 series Gran Coupe in Sanremo Green Metallic with black full merino leather interior**. To be fair, she acknowledged, it was kind of hard to miss.

She dashed across the road, dodging the traffic such as it was (Mr Rowntree's old Bedford van and Mrs Robinson's milk float) then ran along the street to the green BMW car that was parked there. But Mr Benjamin James was not in the car and, it appeared, he was nowhere to be seen. He seemed to have just totally vanished from the face of the Earth.

Hazel looked all around her, at the people across the street, at the two further cars driving past. She started wondering where Mr James had gone to and worrying in case, by some awful twist of fate, that green BMW wasn't his and he had already driven away. She knew what the car looked like, but she didn't notice the number plate, so she couldn't be absolutely definite that the car she was standing next to actually belonged to Mr James, although she'd never seen another one like it in the village.

Then a movement caught her eye and, just as she began to look around behind her, Mr Benjamin James emerged from behind a lamp post.

"What kept you?" he asked.

"You knew I'd come after you?" she panted, out of breath more from the fear that he'd gone and left her again than the exertion of running after him.

"No, I wouldn't say I knew exactly," he explained and shrugged, "But I really kind of hoped you would. So, I thought I'd give you the chance by hanging around here and waiting for you."

He admitted soulfully, "I was starting to get really worried that you weren't going to follow after me though."

Hazel giggled and shook her head as she raised her eyes to the sky. Then she held her right hand out to him and confessed, "My Mum said if I didn't run after you and snap you up, she would do it herself."

Mr James, Benjamin, gave a real laugh, a hearty chuckle and his eyes twinkled at her again. "She's obviously got good taste, your Mum," he quipped.

Hazel smiled and nodded in agreement. "Yes, it looks as if she has," she said as she continued holding her hand out to him.

He returned her smile as he took hold of the hand she'd offered, lifted it up and brushed his lips across the backs of her fingers, which sent a tingle through her and properly set that glow beaming brightly inside her again.

But this time, she didn't mind at all that the glow was there inside her and she didn't even think for one moment of trying to put it out as it grew stronger and stronger, beginning to thoroughly thaw out the heart she'd kept firmly frozen since she realised precisely what Adam had done to her.

She smiled as Mr James, Benjamin, *my* Benjamin as she now gave herself permission to think of him, put his arm around her and hugged her to him, holding her close, tucked under his arm, where she seemed to fit just perfectly.

When Benjamin looked down at her, she moved her gaze from his warm, sparkling brown eyes to his lips. She might have known they'd be full and kissable. Men like him always had full and kissable lips, that's one of the things that make them so dangerous. But, what the heck, this time she was more than prepared to take the risk and hopefully enjoy it.

He moved towards her but stopped, just a few inches away from her face, to make sure it was what she wanted then, when she smiled and nodded to say that was very much what she wanted, he moved in to give her a long and lingering kiss which made her go weak at the knees, as she kind of already knew it would.

Benjamin James kissed her once more, just for good measure, and then he confessed, "Crumbs, I'm so relieved that you came running after me. Even though Alice swore to me that you'd be delighted to see me, I really wasn't at all convinced that you would be. Especially after you'd walked away and left me standing there like a twit in the office. I was determined I was going to give you the pendant for Christmas though, if I did nothing else. You so deserved it and it looks even more beautiful when you're wearing it."

"Oh, thank you, that's so kind of you," said Hazel, gazing up at him. "And I'm sorry for leaving you standing there in the office like that. I was just so mad when I thought I saw you with another girl. I'm so glad that it turned out to be your sister."

"I'm just pleased you believed me," admitted Mr James. "Though I can ring Tanya and ask her to speak to you if you like?" he offered.

"No, it's okay, I believe you, I'm sure it was your sister," replied Hazel. Then she told him, "I missed you dreadfully when you went away."

"I missed you too, so much," agreed Benjamin. "And I promise I'll never leave you alone again. Well, not without telling you where I'm going and when I'll be back, at any rate."

"Good, I should hope not," Hazel responded and he hugged her again.

"By the way, do you have any plans for tomorrow, for Christmas Day?" Hazel asked him, as they walked along the street together, arm in arm.

"Oh, you know, I haven't made any plans at all," Benjamin confided. "My sister and my Dad are spending Christmas in York with her fiancé and his family. I told them I was spending my day with a special girl. It kept me going, all those weeks in Canada when I was working so hard, imagining coming back home to see you. Asking you to be my girlfriend for real and spending a wonderful Christmas with you.'

"And, when I tracked you down and you wouldn't speak to me, I really didn't know what I would do. I didn't want to admit to Tanya and my Dad that I'd messed it all up by not clearing things up with you before I went away. But now, it's too late to sort anything out, I'll just have to go back to my apartment and spend this evening and all day tomorrow, all on my own, I guess," he said with as much pathos as the actor in him could muster.

Hazel chortled, "You're a terrible ham actor, Benjamin James. I know you're just wangling for an invitation to stay with us tonight aren't you?"

Benjamin grinned and confessed, "Yes, I am. You see with Dad going to stay with Tanya in York and Alice telling me all about your Christmases in the village, all the friends and family calling around, always an open door, a bed for the night if people need it. I sort of hoped your Mum or maybe one of your other relatives or friends would find a space for me if I managed to persuade you to forgive me for being, what was it your mother called me, a louse?"

"I think she forgave you a lot quicker than I did," pointed out Hazel. "And we do have a spare bedroom," she confessed, "And my Mum will probably never speak to me again if I send you on your way, especially on Christmas Eve."

"Well, we can't have that," replied Benjamin. "We can't have you and your lovely Mum having an argument over me, can we?"

"No, we can't," she agreed. "So it looks as if you'd better come home with me and, besides, Mum's just made fairy cakes and cookies and apple pie. My Mum makes the best apple pie ever."

"Oh, I love fairy cakes and cookies and apple pie – oh and, of course, Christmas," Benjamin admitted.

"Well, you've come to the right place," Hazel told him. "We'll be swapping Christmas Eve presents after tea and, if I know my Mum, she's probably already wrapping some gifts for you. She always keeps a few spares in case we get unexpected guests."

"That sounds wonderful, I love your Mum already," Benjamin said.

"I think the feeling's mutual, as she was promising to snap you up if I didn't," laughed Hazel as they walked back together along the street to the Brookes' dormer bungalow in their little village, miles from anywhere, to enjoy their first Christmas together with her Mum, Dad and little brother.

That warm glow, growing even stronger inside of Hazel, had completely thawed her frozen heart by then and was busy telling her that they would be celebrating many more Christmases with each other in the future. And the way Benjamin held her close, showed her that he felt exactly the same way, as he smiled down at her while his brown eyes crinkled at the sides and twinkled with love.

The End

If you enjoyed Do Me A Favour, please leave me a star rating or even better a review on Amazon

And perhaps take a look at my novels about Ellie Walker and her friends, gritty tales of young people growing up in the North East of England:

Don't Judge a Book, Still Waters Run Deep and You Can Lead a Horse.

Ellie and her friends will return in:

A Stitch in Time …

Thanks for your support

Rose

Printed in Great Britain
by Amazon